Frederic Jesup Stimson

The Sentimental Calendar

Being Twelve Funny Stories

Frederic Jesup Stimson

The Sentimental Calendar
Being Twelve Funny Stories

ISBN/EAN: 9783744751261

Printed in Europe, USA, Canada, Australia, Japan

Cover: Foto ©Andreas Hilbeck / pixelio.de

More available books at **www.hansebooks.com**

THE
SENTIMENTAL CALENDAR

Being Twelve Funny Stories

BY

J. S. OF DALE

" To every kindly-touched and gentle heart
Greeting, in their Lord's name: which is, in Love's "

NEW-YORK
CHARLES SCRIBNER'S SONS
1886

TO

E. B. S.

. *Many of these stories are here printed for the first time. Others have appeared in Lippincott's, The Century, Harper's and the Harvard magazines, and the New York Independent.*

The vignette headings in this volume are from drawings by
F. G. Attwood.

CALENDAR.

ix

Preface.

By the Major.

SHOWING HOW THESE STORIES CAME
TO BE CALLED FUNNY.

T was the Major that gave them the name, and the stories are serious ; that is, I mean them seriously : nor are they the less serious for being short ; or, at least, it seems to me they are not. I think we are all too ready by three-fifths to look upon short stories with a certain contempt, as we do upon short men. Poe was the first man to see otherwise, particularly with reference to poems : but then Poe was a horrid man, most unexemplary ; and sense, while susceptible of gradual absorption, is not exactly catching. It seems to me this is wrong. I think — will the reader gently allow me to drop the "it seems," and "I think," and other cowardly pseudo-politenesses, and say what I have to say bluntly, not forgetting (nor shall I) that it is all only what I think, and what it seems to me, nor calling me presumptuous for plumping out with what little the Lord has put in my head to say? For a man's lies come home to roost, and his nonsense is pricked in the telling ; and there are prigs enough in the world already, as my Dutch cousin will tell you.

Squarely then, these stories have to be taken *cum grano salis — attici —* and be assured, it is the public's fault if they lack seasoning. Who was it said, "The public are but a mess of instruments"? Get into tune, then, mess of instruments that you are, and look for revenge to the critics — trust me to them.

I can well imagine they will tell you that *the gross flippancy of the Preface is but a foretaste of the book, which is alternately trivial and revolting, and wholly devoid of moral sentiment. The tone and manner of treating the serious side of life, where the author has a deeper purpose (as he assures us he sometimes has), is most disagreeable. The influence of such a book can but be wholly bad. It is a mistake to treat even the minor morals*— Now Heaven bless your minor morals, honest gentleman, and protect them ; I am sure I did not mean to hurt them : believe me, I am sorry if I did. I, too, indulge in the luxury of a moral now and then, and can sympathize — although you may not believe it, it is a fact. I do like variety ; and if I break a convention, in a story or two, I leave it to the respectable Jones to pick it up, and patch it together in a story of his own. Jones can do it — trust him for that. His stories are nothing if not conventional — and, after all, the highest use to which you can put a convention is to break it. You can't make an omelet without breaking eggs ; and even Mrs. Grundy looks her best in short petticoat and a mantilla. Moreover, you should have seen Mrs. Grundy when she was a girl.

But to come to my story, which is very funny. Jim said it was very funny — and, indeed, it was a very funny sort of thing for the Major to say : devilish funny to hear at the time, though, somehow or other, we haven't laughed so much at the Major since as we thought we should, and I told the story at a dinner the other day where it fell quite flat. To come to my first story. I confess I am beginning to feel a little timorous. Pity, gentle critics ! I am much more modest than I thought I was ; and it is such a very little story — if I could only introduce it with a joke now ! " A certain Greek philosopher, having invited his friends to witness the burial of a baby—" No, that's been done to death. " Mrs. Easy, when she employed her nurse—" Who's that nudging my elbow ? Great heavens ! — I beg pardon. I was very near committing an impropriety : I assure you it shall not occur again.

Well, then, attempting no more anecdotes, let me impress upon your mind that it was the Major who said this—the Major. And he said it in a certain club in St. James's street, over a glass of claret-cup (for they drink such things in London, Madam, they do indeed ; but then remember that London is in a corrupt monarchy) ; and that is why Jim laughed so, you see, because it was the Major. It was its coming from the Major that gave the peculiar, delicious, aromatic humor to the thing — old Major Brandyball, man about town these forty years, but who will never, I fear, be a man about the town whose streets are jasper and whose gates are pearl, although he already has one foot and an ankle-joint in a gouty grave. You see, Major Brandyball has not only been a fixture in the Oxlip-and-Camphor Club almost since the days of King Billy, flourishing, like the wicked, in a great bay window, but he is a member of the Devils-on-Horseback, and a limb of Satan to boot. The Major used to be rather popular in the club, but now is little more than an empty butt: the young fellows laugh at him, and the old men smile. His conversation years ago was, I suppose, amusing; but now the stream of wit is dried, and little remains but the dams. He is a profane old fellow, not a nice companion for youth; cynical, a retailer of many stories. He takes a practical view of women, and three glasses of brandy-and-water every afternoon before dinner. At which same dinner he eats too much and doesn't drink too little, and his old face grows purple; and then he either falls asleep over the last glass, or he sits awake over many others, and tattles to the casual smoker with a wheeze in his throat, and many obsolete expletives by way of garniture.

Everybody laughs at the Major, and the Major laughs at everything, except after midnight when he gets too heavy. They say he used to have an eye for beauty, but now it is only for wine; and his wrinkled eyelids are netted with purple blood-vessels, and his bald head shines like the red rind of a Dutch cheese. He lives on his stories now, and on his grand-nephew, as he did on his grand-nephew's father and grandfather before him; for the Major was a younger son. All his brothers and his eldest nephew are dead, and the present one doesn't care to show him very much ; so he stays at the Club most of the time. The Major had been a sad dog in his day. He had been in many little affairs. It is sometimes the custom, in these little games, when the one wins the other goes and dies. But the girl it was that died, with the Major ; so, at least, we always supposed, if either did. Was he not here?

The Major is not æsthetic. He knows nothing of literature or art, less of painting ; cares nothing for the beauties of inanimate nature, and not at all for the drama without ballets.

So I was a little surprised when the Major said it was a fine night. We three were sitting at a window ; behind it was a garden, and the moon was shining. It is an unusual thing for the moon to shine in London ; but not half so unusual as it is for the Major to say it is a fine night. In fact, the remark argued a depth of sentiment, not to say sentimentality, on the part of the Major which we had not hitherto suspected. But this is a Sentimental Calendar.

We sat for some minutes in silence, overcome by this lyric flight ; and then Jim rose and said he had an engagement. He did not say what it was ; but I knew that he was going to see Miss Maberly, Hon. Arthur Maberly's daughter, whom he was going to marry. But the Major broke out again suddenly. "I hear you are engaged to Mary Maberly?" he said. "I remember her grandmother." Jim settled himself in his chair again reluctantly, and waited with much resignation. I composed myself to hear with some apprehension : I had much experience of the Major's stories, and I confess I should not have liked to hear the Major treat the Club to any reminiscences of the grandmother of a girl I was going to marry.

"Yes," said the Major, "I remember her." He drank his brandy hastily, and walked to the window and began drumming on the window-pane. He was silent for some time after that. Jim cocked his eye at me and I made signs at him to get away, fearing some unpleasantness, for there was no telling what yarn the Major might be up to. The Major, however, still stood there, drumming on the glass, and looking out into the moonlight in the garden. Then he broke out, savagely.

"'Tis forty years ago ; but, damme, sir, I remember how that moonlight out there looked, as it shone upon her yellow hair."

That was all. But it was the funniest story the Major ever told. Jim and I got out of the room as best we could, and left the old boy drumming on the window-pane, and thinking of the moonshine, and how it fell upon her yellow hair.

January.

The Bells of Avalon.

STORY TOLD IN A WINTER STORM AT SEA.

ONCE happened to go to Prince Edward's Island.

Some years ago — I am sorry to say that it was some years ago — we had a great rush of business at the office of Messrs. Mugg, Graves & Doggett, attorneys and counselors-at-law. It was at the time of the repeal of the third national bankrupt act ; and the insolvent laws of our State, which is an honest State, being strict, many enterprising firms who had hardly yet had time to fail rushed headlong into bankruptcy while they could still pay a dividend of fifteen per cent. in deferred payments, without prejudice to their right of doing the same thing again at some future time — and probably at the earliest possible one. As much of this business came through our office, we had a very prosperous season ; but by the early summer I was nearly tired out, and the doctors sentenced me to four weeks' vacation.

It was years since I had taken more than two ; and the summer before I had had none, owing to the absence of Mugg, Graves, or Doggett for eight weeks upon a journey through Europe. So, taking leave of my other two partners (for I do not mean to tell you whether I am Doggett, Graves, or Mugg — it would injure me in the profession), I put two over-coats and a valise on the steamer bound for Halifax.

I do not like the sea. It seems to me a sea-voy-age is just so much taken out of a man's life ; and on this trip it was particularly irksome to me. I was too overworked to read ; and, in fact, I had brought no books or business papers with me. And, for the same reason, I could only smoke in moderation. Moreover, cigars always taste bitter in the sea damp-ness, and I missed the morning and evening papers, which is another marine hardship, and a serious one. I talked a little with the captain — more about marine collisions than anything else, as I had just got one or two admiralty retainers — and arrived in Halifax on the third day.

I judged there was not much business doing at Halifax. All the British possessions in North Amer-ica seem to be in a state of dry rot, commercially speaking. In Halifax it was strikingly so, though the city is well situated upon a fine harbor, and the province produces almost all the valuable raw mate-rials of manufacturing, except cotton. And, after all, cotton manufacturing is being rather overdone with us.

Of course, I drove up to the fort, and heard the band play, and saw a red-coat or two. These British soldiers always produce a sort of irritation in me — the coarse, animal-looking privates ; the insolent officers, with their ridiculous little caps stuck on the side of their heads, and their general self-sufficient, we-own-the-universe manner of bearing themselves. In short, Halifax made no impression upon me other than to arouse a sort of contemptuous pity coupled with a strong desire to get away ; so I got away. I don't know why I went to Prince Edward's Island ; but I came by Truro, and so to Pictou, and then, naturally enough, crossed over to Charlottetown. It is a stunted little town ; flat, with wide, straight streets, unoccupied warehouses, and a parliament house, reminding one of some ordinary middle-aged citizen, who has settled himself, after his youthful dreams of importance are over, to a placid domestic insignificance in a second-rate city. I got quite used to it in an hour or two, and wandered about familiarly enough in the grassy streets, as if I belonged there, feeling no longer in any particular hurry. I had been a week without a live newspaper, and it seemed perfectly natural to saunter up at sunset to what they called the park, and look out over the bay ; or to idle through the grounds of the official residence of His Excellency, the Governor, in the company of a garrulous old gardener who took great pride in his peas and beans, and finally bade me admire, in a very triumph of climax, a group of fairish-sized trees near the house — "the finest trees in the island, sir."

"Lindens?" said I.

"No, sir; no, sir. They are planes."

I looked at them — they seemed to me ordinary lindens enough — and gave him sixpence for the show. I suppose, in that Arctic climate, anything of size, that is not a fir or pine, is a rarity. Still, I walked back to town, rather enjoying it all. The streets were filled with young men and women, making love in a leisurely sort of way, as if courtship were the one excitement of life and 'twere a pity to get it all over too quickly. I was rather surprised at being no more bored than I was; but my mind seemed to be in a sort of vacuous, pensive state. I take it this is why doctors recommend a change of scene, and why we find rest in travel. I slept uncommonly well that night.

I got up late the next day,— it was a Sunday,— so late that it seemed hardly worth while to go off walking in the hour or two of the morning that remained before dinner. Charlottetown was differ ent from Halifax. Perhaps it was so obviously impossible for the place ever to be flourishing that I did not think to worry about it. It is not unpleasant to be lonely, in a lazy sort of sadness; and, after dinner, I left the town, and walked along by the sea; or, rather, by the arm of the bay which stretches up above the town. In an hour the little city was out of sight — my guide-book placed its population at only eight thousand — and I was walking by a marshy shore, the salt water rising through the clayey beach at every footstep. Shoreward was a gentle hill, crowned with a few low trees. How pretty a thick-leaved oak can be, with the cattle lying under it in the shade! It had been a hot noontide, and most things seemed asleep. There was a simple kind of beauty in the land: it was flat, but fertile, cultivated; not wild and rocky, like New England. There was a spring of water, coming up clear through the brown sand, close by the salt water's edge. I drank of it. It was slightly brackish, but cold, and not unpleasant. Then I had to follow up a brook, in a little soft ravine of pasture land. It was half brook, half sea-creek; but at its source I found this, too, came bubbling out of the earth. Just here the country was really beautiful, or it seemed so to me, fresh from the office; and I lay awhile under another oak, and looked at it. There was no house in sight now; but one brick gable was visible in the distance, rising from a wood on a point of land which jutted out into the bay ahead of me.

I had been walking on along the beach an hour or more toward this (which was farther off than I had thought it) when I saw an old man shambling over the stones toward me. He was very poorly dressed, with no hat, and nothing but an old pair of slippers on his feet, which slipped and slid upon the round pebbles. I was going by him with a nod ; but he stopped as if to speak to me, with a puzzled expression upon his face.

"Is this — is this Avalon?" said he.

"Avalon?" said I.

He looked at me intently, and yet with an empty, distant gaze, as if I were hardly real to him. A suspicion came to me that the man was mad, and I shrank back.

"Avalon?" said I. "Avilion?"— for something made me think, as I stood looking at him, of that fabled island of the blest in the sea.

"No, no," said he, impatiently. "Avalon. Avalon — in Newfoundland, you know."

Then I remembered the peninsula of Avalon, near St. John's, in Newfoundland ; the ship cannot be far from there to-day.

"Oh! Avalon," I answered. "No. This is not Avalon."

The old man's face fell, and he turned away. "They all say the same," he muttered. "They all say the same. They are mad." Again I thought of my first notion, and I saw his face grow dull again, and empty, with the look of halting feebleness that old insane people often have. Beyond me was the great brick building, barrack-looking, with irons in the windows. It was evidently the insane asylum of the province, and this was one of the inmates, escaped, perhaps, an old man like him, from their watching.

" Oh ! " said he quickly, as if he read my thoughts.
" They let me walk alone, sometimes." I saw that
he was harmless.

" Why did you think it was Avalon, my friend ? "
I said gently, for something in his sadness interested me.

At the word he looked up eagerly. " Avalon,
Avalon," said he ; " I heard the bells." And truly,
there had been church-bells ringing in the afternoon.

" And why do you wish for Avalon ? " I asked
him.

" My wife is there, sir," said the old man, simply.
" And we were to go there to live when I had bought
the house. But they will not let me now."

" But t is is in Prince Edward's Island ? "

I did not know then what I could have said to
bring tears into the poor man's eyes ; but he sat
down wearily, and I could see that he was crying.

" Yes," he said. " Oh ! I remember." And the
vacant look had gone now from them, and left alone
the weary one of sorrow. So I asked, and sitting
down with him, I got his story. It came, mingled
with querulous complaints at his food, and with the
way his keepers treated him, and with senile, petty
spites, and broken sequences of story ; but now and
then, when his mind was with him (and in such
times his mood was saddest, and his tears would
come again), he told it clearly. So simple a story is
hardly worth the telling ; but it is fresh in my mind,
as if it were but yesterday.

It seems he had been born in Avalon; the name
of the place he had forgotten—"but you know,
sir," said he, "the village on the cliff there, by the
little church?" And I told him that I knew it well.
He had followed the sea, of course; and in due time
(of course) he fell in love. Anne, I remember, was
her name. But Newfoundland is a savage place in
which to live; so he had gone to sea, and had been
a wild fellow in his time, as he gave me, in his simple
way, to know. His wild way had been but simple,
too—a little overdrinking, perhaps, to keep out the
cold; a careless way of treating church, and such like
matters. Then, finally, he had known Anne; or,
more likely, he had known her as a child; but in the
end he had married her. Then he had gone to sea
again, to win enough to buy a little land at home, in
Avalon, and build a home for her there. "But the
money had been ower slow in coming, sir"; and
years had passed and seen them little farther toward
the farm in Avalon. But still, at home there, she
kept spinning and saving what she could toward it,
and he kept following the sea.

At last he got a chance for higher wages than a
common seaman's; it was in the mail service, sailing
the boat from Prince Edward's Island to the mainland.
In the summer it was well enough; but in the winter,
when the ice-floes blocked the strait, it was a terrible
life. Ofttimes the boat had to be dragged, or the ice-
boat sailed, for miles over the frozen sea; crossing

now the open water, now huge fields of ice piled up, with the terrible winter storms, and the snows, and the chance of being carried out to sea. Anne had been loath to have him take to the life from the first ; but he had talked to her of Avalon, and the little white house and patch of land for their old age, and so he had persuaded her. She had gone with him to Prince Edward's Island, though, and lived there, that she might be with him half the time at least ; and even this was better than the long sea-voyages. And perhaps, too, his being " but a wild lad " had had a bit to do with that ; " for you know, sir, we sailor men are ower like to take to drink on shore, with nothing there to do but sit and see our mates about their grog. But I always kept straight, sir, over there on the mainland. Any man would do that, you know, sir, with such a wife as Anne." And every voyage he made was something added to the little store that was to buy the house in Avalon. " But she always had a fear of them winter voyages, sir. The women, they never can get used to the sea ; partic'lar those up our way, as sees so much of what the sea can do. But I was doing finely, sir, and Anne, she was going to have a baby; and we almost felt as if the house were ready bought, just by the little church there, in the pastur' field. It was the second or third winter ; and it was an awful cold one, sir ; and then — "

Again the empty stare of his insanity came in his eyes, and he sat silent, nodding his head slowly.

"And then —" I prompted.

"And then — it was in March, I think, sir — I was over on the mainland ; and we had been there nigh onto a week, and the ice it was so broken and so bad we couldn't 'a' got back, sir, for the life of us. But a schooner had got across from the island arter we left ; and I knew a man on board, — Sandy Fraser, you know, sir, o' Pictou, — and he brought word as how my wife war ill. And I knew the baby was a-coming about that time, and I was nigh crazy, sir, for to get back.

"An' I used to walk down on the shore, sir, and wish as how the ice would break and go, and look over through the thick weather and try to see the island, and think how Anne might be a-doin'. An' the mates they used to sit around the stove an' tak' their grog, and laugh at me for being so anxious like. An' at last there came a day that there warn't but half a gale a-blowin' ; an' I up an' swore I'd go back, sir. An' the mates, they all said I war crazy ; but there was a couple as said they'd go, seein' as I thought we could do it. And the mail was all ready, and had been waitin' for days ; and it seemed as if I could hear Anne a-callin'.

"And in the mornin' we started from Cap' Tourmentine — three men in the boat, and the mail-bags. An' that day we made out fairly well ; we might 'a' got half-way across before the sundown. But in the night it came up warm from the sou'east ; and all the ice began to break up with the sea an' go out. I never

see such a storm as were that; an' the ice war all in
pieces, chunk-like. First we had a drag, an' then a
swim; an' so on every quarter mile or so. An' in
the mornin' it war terrible cold again, an' all our
garmints they were stiff as boards with the wet, an'
then with the freeze. An' the boat war all broke up
with a squeeze we got in the blow; and next night
we had to break up the ship, and burn the timbers,
or we would ha' froze. An' one man froze his foot;
an' both my ears were that solid, sir, they'd ha'
broke if you bent 'em. But I thought o' Anne, an'
the little house in Avalon, an' the baby, an' I kept
on. An' then, the next day, we had to take to the
ice altogether, an' we left the ship, half burnt as she
was. But we saw the coast ahead, near by Summer-
side; only there was a widish bit o' water, where
the field ice had broke loose from the shore. An' the
ice was breakin' up where we war; an'—an' we had
to jump into the sea, an' it was awful cold; an' they
put out from the shore in boats—the men did; and
when we got there, they all said as how—leastwise,
I disremember—I must ha' been fever-like a spell;
but when I came to, they told me Anne was dead;
an' they never let me see her; an' then—an' then
they brought me here—" The old man broke off suddenly, as if he forgot his story.

"Is this Avalon?" he asked again.

"No," I said; "not yet."

I saw that he was crazy. When he next spoke it
was fretfully.

" An' they keep me here, nor won't let me go home. An' they don't give me enough to eat, sir ; not always. It's a shame, in a Christian country. And they treat me like as if I were foolish ; kind o' old an' foolish. An' now they'll be after me, for stayin' out so long."

And so his mind began to wander in senile complaining once more ; and, after a few broken sentences, he became quiet, and looked across the bay. The sun was just setting, over by a distant rim of land ; and the broad sea-water lay smooth and silent, yellow in the glow, like molten gold. Suddenly the old man put his hand to his ear and gazed far over at the sunset, listening intently, with the same expression I had first noticed in his eyes. They looked, unshaded, at the light, his face brightening in the last rays of the sun ; and I forgot his madness and his rags in watching the one look of perfect happiness I have ever seen on a human face.

" Avalon !   The bells of Avalon ! " he whispered. "Do you hear them, Anne?   The bells of Avalon —"

I looked away, across the yellow sea ; and, listening, it seemed that I, too, heard the bells.

February.

Mr. Pillian Wraye, Agnostic Necromancer.

TO BE READ AFTER THE LAST BALL, LATE IN
SHROVE-TUESDAY NIGHT.

Some months since Mr. Pillian Wraye went off and lived nine weeks in a hermitage, owing to the prevalence of fools. The manner of this was as follows :

Mr. Pillian Wraye was, and is still, a young man of poetical imagination, and of some social success. At times he is possessed of high ambitions, and fancies that he would like to perform great and noble things ; and he always has cards to the most exclusive entertainments in New-York. He is frequently not without a feeling for the true and the beautiful, and is a member of both the Union and the Knickerbocker clubs. I do not think I understate it when I say that often, when he dines alone in the large hall of the former establishment, he is infused with the spirit of Poesy, and has thoughts of mystical romance. At such times his aspirations are positively transcendental. His lowest desires are those of an Endymion or an Epaminondas. By the end of his pint of Pommard, he really does not know whether to die for his country, or to live and illustrate it with his own glory. These thoughts adorn his loneliness, and he becomes conscious of his superiority to the other men in the hall who are dining in company and telling stories.

Mr. Wraye is not in business, not liking trade. His father succeeded, during his highly respectable career, in selling so considerable a quantity of commodities for more than they were worth, that Pillian is now enabled to command the labor of some seven-and-twenty American citizens, at the current average price of one dollar sixty-two and a half cents a day, without a *quid pro quo* of personal exertion on his own part. To speak more conventionally, in the inexact but popular mode of expression, he has sixteen thousand a year.

Pillian has been called odd; or, perhaps, wild would better describe it. His late father once or twice accused him of raising the devil. But this exaggeration of Pillian's powers must be ascribed to paternal pride: his wild oats, after all, were but a very domestic article, and are now all sown. But still, in speech if not in action, Wraye has a way of running counter to the respectable canons of brown-stone-front ethics which must inevitably excite the prejudices of those whose means do not permit eccentricity. Wraye's income does not depend on the opinion of his fellow-men, and an income has been well defined to be the mainspring of modern life and the dayspring of the occidental soul.

It was only last winter that Wraye resolved to raise the devil in due earnest. He had been lunching;

there was no one in the morning-room but Van
Buskirk, in his accustomed seat by the fire. Wraye,
who had been feeling rather poor lately, was drinking
Macon ordinaire. It may be that the Macon was not
so good as the Pommard ; it may be that Wraye was
out of sorts, and, consequently, his life lacked variety.
But things in general seemed to him in a bad way ;
and after lunch Van Buskirk asked him to take some
brandy, which did not mend them. Then Van Buskirk went off to his billiards or some other device for
attaining earthly happiness, and Wraye grew blue.
He had had four months of that New-York life which
our naturalist-novelists, as if it were some rare beetle,
are striving so earnestly to impale. But Wraye was
thinking the result would still be mush, through
whichever part of it you stuck a pin.

The fact is, Wraye was a man who had long since
grasped the world in its universality and found it too
small by half. And as for that part of the world
which calls itself the World, and is ordinarily in a
partnership with the Flesh and the Devil, Wraye had
become convinced that it was often unnatural and
sometimes insincere. He thirsted for the truth, for
the reality of nature, not the realism of fiction ; for
the normal changes of the seasons as opposed to
abnormal fashions and enormities of art. So he went
off and passed nine weeks in a cabin, where, as has
been said, he kept himself much to himself, owing to
the prevalence of fools.

Not that this cabin was in a vast contiguity of folly.
It was but a little lonely stone hut, with a hangar, and

it nestled on the shaggy shoulder of one of the highest of the mountains of the Great Smoky range. It was far removed from any town, lost among the mountain laurels and the flowering rhododendron ; and therein Wraye, having due leisure, gave himself up to the practice of all the Christian virtues, save humility alone, which was, of course, impracticable in that lonely place, and is not, perhaps, much easier in any other.

I said that Mr. Wraye resolved to raise the devil, but it was but an afterthought and happened in this wise. When he thus abandoned his habits as a man in society, and flew off on a tangent in search of the normal, he began by taking a ferry-boat for Jersey City ; and the last thing he did in Manhattan was to go to Mr. Burton's book-store on Fifth Avenue (you remember it has a gilt owl over the door), where he bought the last French novel, some books on German metaphysics, and a few odd volumes in rare bindings which Mr. Burton's clerk threw in, thinking Wraye would never look at them, while they could charge well for them in the bill. And Wraye did not look at them again, except only the first chapter of one of the German philosophers, which proved satisfactorily that nothing extraneous could possibly exist unless you had a very confident high opinion of yourself. Wraye got as far as this between Newark and Trenton, but he read no further ; and for many days after his arrival at the mountain the books lay unopened on the floor, and served only as a pedestal for his tobacco-jar. Wraye, thinking the location extremely attractive, had hired the cabin of a slab-sided Georgian and abandoned himself entirely to the Christian virtues.

After two weeks on a mountain-top in south-eastern Tennessee—it is a sad and very painful thing thing to tell—but after fourteen days on a mountain-top smothered in laurels and with a view only into Cherokee county, N. C., Wraye found that some of the Christian virtues began to pall. When they once began to pall, they palled rapidly. It was not that the rôle of St. Simeon Stylites was unfashionable—by his occasional disregard for fashion (a part of the eccentricity I mentioned before) Wraye had long since shaken to the foundation the intimacy of his most trusted friends, to say nothing of their sisters' mothers—it was not that it was unfashionable, but it was so terribly ineffective. Some of our most unctuous preachers, on top of a pole, and silent at that, would be failures most signal.

Now, Wraye hated to be ineffective. By this time he was in the eighty-second latitude, as it were, of the True and Beautiful; but what was the practical profit of gripping their very essence if he could not show it to others? What was the use of being a great man all alone by himself, his friends not seeing it? Upon closely analyzing this last sentiment, Wraye did not feel sure that there was not a bit of dross in the gold it unquestionably contained. This discovery threw him into a fit of depression, which he endured for seven days and six nights. On the seventh night he decided to leave the Christian virtues and go in for necromancy.

In these days it has grown to be the fashion to doubt the possibility of raising the devil except in the usual and figurative sense. Possibly this is owing to the unfortunate use of the verb *raise,* which implies the bringing him from a lower to a higher place. There are many localities where the devil himself could hardly be expected to arrive soaring. Obviously, he could not thus reach New-York. Be that as it may, Wraye was on a mountain-top and felt no difficulty there. And as to the other and general impossibility, Wray easily dismissed it from his mind. In the first place, the devil had often been successfully evoked in the middle ages, and the thing had not, of late, been fairly tried ; in the second place, Wraye had almost, if not quite, succeeded in practicing all the Christian virtues, which must surely be a far more difficult thing to do. Lastly (and this is the difficulty which commonly troubles Bostonians), Wraye's father was a good Calvinist, and had brought him up to fear God and have faith in the devil ; or at all events (for this does not seem to be the proper antithesis) to believe in the devil. Despite his agnostic tendencies, Wraye had hitherto seen no reason whatever to doubt the devil's existence. And, indeed, I doubt if any one can, who does not live with his own personality on terms of daily polite fictions.

Wraye had been alone with himself three
weeks when he came to this strange resolve. **II. THE**
FLESH.
It was then late in the afternoon of a gray
Monday. Throughout the morning the sun had struggled to reach the earth, but at last the mists had pre-
vailed. Above, the clouds moved in dense bodies,
shrouding the sky ; but below Wraye's cabin they
were frayed and straggling, and, through frequent
rifts, he could see dark mountain forms. Huge lean
pines rose up from the chilly wreaths of cloud and
stretched their gaunt arms toward him. There is
something weird, fantastic, about great pines, the
hemlocks of Scandinavia, the *sapins* which shade the
pages of old Alsatian story. Wraye was minded of
these, and of ancient Druid forests, and the wooded
solitude of the Carpathians.

There are seven devils which may be evoked on
the seven separate days, according to the mighty
invocation of good Pope Honorius. Wraye thought
best to invite them all ; he did not wish to be exclusive ; and he learned the method from one of the
books his bookseller had sold him — a small fifteenth-
century treatise on the black art, written in Latin and
bound in vellum.

He built his fire of moss, twigs, and brush, then
of huge sections and segments of forest trees now
moldering on the mountain-side ; trees that were sap-
lings when Tannhaüser entered the haunted mountain
in Thuringia and lost his soul. The chimney was
wide, but hardly wide enough to carry off the vol-

umes of smoke, smelling of earth and decay, that
rose from this dissolution too quickly made.   The
floor of flat stones, and the walls, and even the windows and roof, he quilted with scarlet cloth ; so that
all light, even by day, came from the fire and one
small lamp burning animal oil.   It took him a day's
journey and a night's work to make all the preparations ; but by the next night he had his caldron
ready, containing the eyes of an owl, the blood of
a snake, the heart of a raven, and other necessary
ingredients.   At such a distance from the city, he
could not get all that his book told him he must
have — a woman's glove for instance, and the heart
of a girl ; but by way of making it up, he threw in
an old volume of Herbert Spencer.

The magic circle must either be drawn with char-
coal and holy water, or a piece of the wood of the
true cross.   Wraye used the former, as being more
easy to procure ; and in the circle he inscribed the
double super-imposed triangle, at the six points of
which he placed dinner-cards, on which were written
respectively the names of the six expected guests —
Asmodeus and Mephisto, Beelzebub and Belphegor,
Astaroth and Abaddon.   The name of Lucifer was
inscribed in the center, with the invitation, in the
names ineffable of On, Alpha, Ya, Reg, Sol, and
Ingodum.   Around the circle he wrote : *By the name
thou bearest, Lucifer, enter not within this circle.*
Having now made all ready, Wraye himself entered
within the circle, the caldron having begun to boil.

The books say that when you enter you must wear nothing impure, and only carry gold and silver ; but Wraye thought it safer, on the whole, to leave his silver dollars behind, being Bland's, and he threw a gold one on the floor for Nambroth to pick up, while he pronounced the words *Alpha, Omega, Ely, Elohe, Zebahot, Elion, Saday.*

You may say what you like about devils, but most men, finding themselves, by a tempestuous March midnight, alone on the peak of one of the Great Smoky Mountains, in a room hung in red cloth, with the signs of the Zodiac and other disreputable characters on the walls, and a broth in which the most prominent feature is a human skull brewing in the caldron, and, to put it in its mildest light, only a strange mathematical diagram to sit in (and Wraye always hated mathematics) — most men would have been uncomfortable. A solitary cook makes the broth too effective, they might fear.

Not so our hero. He would have welcomed any one but an acquaintance. He would have reveled in anything but the ordinary course of nature. Apparitions would have charmed him, and specters would have delighted his soul. Nambroth, who is a sort of valet-de-chambre to Asmodeus, ordinarily appears between nine and ten in the evening ; but so far was Wraye from being overcome by possibilities that he had great difficulty in keeping awake. And hardly had his traveling-clock with the cathedral chime struck the last stroke of ten, when he fell asleep,

with his head on the vellum-bound book ; and the
night passed according to all the laws laid down in
Ganot's physics, while Wraye dreamed that he was
paying a party-call on a lady in East Thirty-sixth
street.

As the dawn was not visible through the scarlet
cloth, Wraye woke up very late in the morning.
His first care was the fire, which had not gone out,
one big sycamore trunk keeping it well preserved.
The contents of the kettle were low and needed
replenishing. Wraye walked out on the mountain-
top ; the view was superb. It was a beautiful morning, and a large section of one of our free and
independent States was spread at his feet. A little
curl-paper of white smoke afar off came from a train
on the East Tennessee, Virginia, and Georgia Railroad, in the preferred stock of which company Wraye
had lately made an unfortunate speculation. The
subject was a painful one ; and he carried his eyes
upward to the blue sky. High above was a bald
eagle, turning and soaring in the air, now but a black
spot, now a white speck in the sunlight. He was a
noble bird ; and Wraye brought his rifle from the
hut, sighted hastily, and fired. The creature's career
was suddenly checked. He fell, and in a few seconds crashed in the shrubs, dead, at Wraye's feet.
Wraye was not ordinarily a good shot, and this
occurrence gave him food for reflection.

But it was necessary to bestir himself about the
caldron. Laying the carcass of the eagle in one

corner of the shanty, he set forth on his long journey down the mountain. For the first mile or two, the path was a mere opening in the jungle of rhododendron ; then he entered a solemn hemlock forest, and followed the course of a roaring torrent. He looked about him with watchful eyes, but felt that he could hardly expect anything very unusual to happen in broad daylight, even among the pines. Besides, the air and exercise made his spirits buoyant, and not at all in a mood sympathetic to supernatural visitors.

The walk took him many hours, and it was late in the afternoon when he returned with the things he had been in search of. He was tired in body, and inclined to be heavy in spirit. The way in places was bordered by trees that had died when Richelieu was Cardinal; now mere trunks, stripped of their bark, smooth and silvery — white like bones. The twigs stretched out across his path, and in one of them he saw, in the twilight, an owl. The bird looked at him seriously as he passed. This seemed promising.

Surely something might be expected to happen that night. It was, of course, too early for the devil to appear in person ; but it would be no more than courteous for him to send some sort of avant-courier of his coming. Wraye tried to remember what happened in Der Freischütz when the first bullet was cast. There was an owl on a stump, that he was sure of ; the owl had a red eye, and the stump wobbled ; and then, he was not sure, but he thought he remembered a platoon of ravens coming down from the sky in a sort of net-work, and after that, of course, the wild huntsman might be expected to turn up. Wraye had a very terrible incantation, indeed, set down for that night; and it was Abaddon's day for receiving, who, as his name implies, is one of the worst of devils. Abaddon comes from the very depths of the pit; and by the time Wraye had repeated his incantation, and got himself well within the triangles, he really began to feel himself on terms of acquaintance with almost any of the powers below.

But that night, and the next, and the next after that, and even the first week, all passed without any occurrence worthy to be called a happening. Every periapt and cantrap known to the thaumaturge was employed by Wraye in vain. Aeromancy, bousanthropy, cleromancy, daphnomancy, engastrimism, fatalism, gyromancy, hepatoscopy, illuminism, kinematics, lithomancy, magic, omphalomancy, palingenesis, quietism, rhabdomancy, sciamancy, theurgy, utesetury, vampirism, will, xylomancy, hyloscopy, and zairagia were all used to no purpose. Wraye began to be rather more bored than he had been in New-York. This was far from a proper frame of mind. Then the mountain life had much improved his health, and given him a most unconscionable appetite. This was a most discouraging symptom. He racked his brains, but could remember no recorded instance of the devil's appearing to any man whose chief anxiety was about getting something to eat.

Wraye was growing fat, and would have been well contented but for the slight put upon him by the infernal powers. It was not agreeable to think that Satan did not deem him of sufficient importance to keep the appointment ; and it was even humiliating to suspect that his soul was not considered worth the purchasing. True, you might say, there was uncommonly little for Satan to do in the mountains. It was hardly worth his while to go so far afield to bag a single bird. To be sure, the natives did very little work ; there were plenty of idle hands ; but then they had no ambition whatever, and even the devil found no work for these to do. By that sin fell the angels. These were mostly poor white trash, quite without any pomps and vanities. They scratched around and raised a little corn in the spring, but sat for the most of the year with their hands in their pockets, being of opinion that a square loaf was distinctly better than wheaten bread. One man was very little better than another, and all the women were on terms of calling acquaintance. What was Satan to do in such a society?

Many days passed, and Wraye really began to doubt whether the other side would come to time. You could hardly expect the devil, a city man, to leave town in the height of the season, and enjoy a country visit. It would be terribly dull for him. The third week had now been passed by Wraye, every night in his magic circle, the fire, duly burning, never having gone out. By this time he

ought, by rights, to have seen the Flying Dutchman,
the Flying Huntsman, Venus Verticordia, and several
packs of hounds, to say nothing of bengal lights and
green fire; and there should have been no end of
were-wolves, kobolds, and such-like spectral small
fry. Every day he had scrupulously put each new
and nastier mixture in the caldron, and although the
resulting mixture had each time been attended by a
new and nastier smell, not the slightest odor of brim- .
stone had yet been perceptible. His own plumpness
was really distressing, and he had run out of tobacco.
He began to take a singular pleasure in his outdoor
life and the scenery; and this, conjoined with the
fact that he was wholly free of the blues, made him
fear that the devil was hardly very near, even yet.
Wraye could not but feel that he had committed himself too strongly on the side of the Christian virtues
before beginning.

Now and then, to be sure, business seemed to be
looking up a little. One foggy day, in the fourth
week, Wraye fell in with a little devil on horseback,
and gave chase. The imp rode like a centaur; and
as they thundered down the rocky pass, the spectral
steed struck a stream of sparks from every hoof, and
Wraye felt much doubt whether his horse, being
mortal, was the more sure-footed. At last he over-
hauled the gnome, and grasped the horse by his rope
bridle; but the little rider slipped off on the grass,
and, beginning to cry, begged Wraye not to hurt him,
and swore that he would find all the letters in the

bag. Questioned as to his nature and identity, the boy asserted himself to be the United States mail, and, finding his captor amicable, promptly demanded ten cents to supplement his salary. Wraye relinquished the coin demanded, and walked home crestfallen.

I have only described his overtures to Nambroth and Abaddon ; but his attempts with Acham, Bechet, Nabam, Aquiel, and even with the higher nobility, like Astaroth and Belphegor, were equally unsuccessful. On one occasion, it being Aquiel's Sunday out, Wraye was out botanizing among the shrubbery, when he saw a tall figure peering at him from behind a volcanic rock. The figure was clothed in red, with black legs, carrying a very straight tail between them. Its face was distinctly black, and Wraye promptly rushed after it. The figure bounded over the rocks with the most tremendous strides, and finally disappeared in a cleft in the side of the mountain. A nimbus of smoke still marked the spot where it had vanished ; and upon arriving there, Wraye found a group of illicit distillers making applebrandy. They all wore red flannel shirts and high boots, and each was lying on the ground, smoking a pipe, with a long rifle between his legs. They had sent one of their number out as a spy, with blackened face, to see what in Tennessee the pesky revenue-officer was doing in their vicinity. They had taken Wraye for a revenue-officer because he wore a pot hat. " No man but one o' them Gov'nment

fellers ever wears a b'iled shirt in these parts," said
they. "An' if he warn't an officer, what was he
after Jim so for?"

Wraye could hardly tell them he had taken Jim for
the devil; but he took so deep a potation of their
own apple-jack as to convince even Jim of his inno-
cence. And when he woke up the next morning,
pondering upon this occurrence, he did not even have
a headache. There was not much in this to encourage him. They were sinning, to be sure, but only
against the United States Revised Statutes. He could
scarcely expect the devil to care very much about
that, when he had the whole New-York Custom-house
to attend to. The fact is, Wraye was rapidly becom-
ing discouraged. It was a Monday, and the forty-
eighth day of the seven weeks. He looked up at the
eagle, which a hunter named Jenkins had stuffed for
him and he had nailed over the door; but the countenance of the eagle was lifeless and inexpressive.
Even an eagle can be inexpressive, when nailed over
a door-way. He looked down again at his magic
circle. All the names had been rubbed out save
Lucifer. This was Lucifer's day. For h:m he had
a conjuration of the most awful potency, good for all
hours of the day and night. Wraye repeated it,
and then, looking out of the window, saw a pretty
girl.

This was the last thing he had expected to see;
but Wraye was an old bird, and ready for the devil in
any shape. He walked out and entered into conver-

sation with her. He could not help feeling that, while she was pretty enough for anything, the stuff of her dress had never seen any place nearer hell than Manchester ; and the devil should really have shown better taste than to have had it cut by a milliner in East Tennessee. However, there was no one to see them on the summit of the Great Smoky Mountains, and Wraye walked along beside her. After winding a few hundred yards down the bald mountain-side, the path enters the great hemlock forest. In this Wraye and his companion disappeared, and were lost to view from the stone cabin. The fire, now forty-nine days old, blazed on ; the day waned ; the contents of the caldron steamed lower ; the night came on ; the eagle remained nailed over the door ; but of the bold exorcist nothing more was seen — or would have been, had anything with eyes remained.

Meantime, our hero had elicited the following facts from the pretty girl : she was a member of the Methodist Episcopal Church ; she lived in Ducktown, Tenn.; she was engaged to be married to Bill Jenkins ; she had been over the mountain to order the wedding-cake, and, coming back, she had lost her way. The marriage being fixed for the same evening, this was unfortunate, and she had stopped at Wraye's cabin to ask him the way, the smoke from his incantations being visible for some distance.

Wraye put her on the right path, and she gratefully invited him to the wedding. Being a personal acquaintance of the groom (Bill Jenkins, in fact, had stuffed his eagle), Wraye accepted. They all had a very pleasant night of it, without any shooting. Jenkins was a capital fellow, and they ended up with a moonlight dance and plenty of moonshine whisky.

It was a very early hour in the morning when Wraye got back to the stone cabin. His fire was out, but had first burned a hole through the bottom of the caldron, and its contents had disappeared in the ashes. He carefully scanned the room ; but there was nothing to show the presence of any visitor, supernatural or otherwise. Even his pipe lay empty where it had been thrown, and a jug of apple-jack, a present from his friends the moonshiners, remained intact. Everything, through seven long weeks, had surely been done in the most correct and careful manner by him ; and Wraye at last felt convinced that Satan was a myth. During the course of the experiment he had grown immoderately fat ; and he would have been very well content with the result, but that he hated to fail in anything, even in an exorcism. It was too late to go to bed, and he sat outside among the rhododendrons, now almost in flower, and watched the dawn. The sunrise over the mountains was very beautiful, far superior to that of the Rigi as Wraye remembered it. He packed up his traps and took the night train for New-York.

When Wraye awoke, he was in a berth in a sleeping-car. A sharp ray of sunlight came through the curtain and lit up a few III. THE DEVIL. million motes, dancing with the motion of the express train. He was reminded of the million souls of enemies which some medieval imagination discovered dancing on the point of a needle. He pulled up the dusty window-curtain, thereby letting free a few billion more such souls, and looked out. The train was bowling over the green floor of the Valley of Virginia. The fields were fresh in such an unwonted slant of sunlight that he saw it must be very early ; the red-clay earth was still stiff with flower-columns and pilasters of frost, destined soon to melt in the sunshine.

All his weeks on the mountain seemed a dream ; most of all, that strange fortnight when he had been so singularly successful with the Christian virtues. As for that last seven, wherein he had renounced the world for the devil and gained so much flesh, they only served to convince him that the devil was a myth. If there ever was one, he had vanished before the keen glance of science like a partridge before a cockney, or a chamois before a Cook's tourist. And Wraye bought a cigar from the porter, and bestowed his twelve stone comfortably in the smoking-car.

Towards midday, the ride growing tedious, Wraye went a step farther and began to doubt the solidity of the Christian virtues themselves. Were not all abstractions the toys of sentimentalists? Science treats of conditions only. Now, an act may be good or bad,—nay, there is something dangerously romantic even in these terms; say, rather, suitable or unsuitable, —an organism may act suitably or unsuitably as regards its environment, but to say that the totality of such acts is good, and— Just here Wraye began to yawn. It was odd how much more he remembered than he had supposed of that book of Herbert Spencer's he had boiled down in the caldron. It had rather bored him when he read it. Halloa—Washington. Realities or dreams, the Christian virtues would have been quite impracticable here. And Wraye remembered with a smile that one of his youthful ambitions had been to go to Congress.

It was an uncommonly long journey to New-York. There was a pretty little Quakeress on the train, but she got out at Philadelphia. What an extremely disagreeable set of people always seemed to be passing through New Jersey! And the climate of the State was always impregnated with peanuts and stale tobacco. Wraye looked through his dressing-bag for his cologne-bottle and something to read. The cologne had an odd smell; it seemed to have grown pungent in the mountains. All his reading matter was a French novel that he had also brought from New-York, and he had kept it ten weeks with uncut pages. Wraye now cut them with a lava paper-knife, and was soon lost in the most iniquitous realisms of modern life. New Jersey flew by him like an unseen vision, and he reached the finis of the novel and the ferry-boat at Jersey City at the same moment.

Wraye had now that comforting self-approbation which springs from the knowledge that there is much wickedness in the world in which one has no share, and that one is not likely to sink so low as the people of whom one has just been reading. This is the ethical ground of reading French novels. He walked, in a superior manner, through the ladies' saloon, and lighted a cigar just beyond the door on the forward deck. It was a fine April night, little colder than in the mountains, notwithstanding his two hundred leagues' journey to the north. In the late twilight a large flock of black birds was visible, high over the bay, flying slowly northward in a curious serried order, as if caught in a net. Wraye wondered if he had lost any good turns in stocks by his absence, and bought an evening paper ; but was happy to find that he had rather gained than lost by being away. He took a carriage at Desbrosses street and gave the direction to his lodgings.

Passing by his bookseller's, it occurred to him, having used up all his literature, that he would drop in and get something to read. As he entered the shop, it struck him that there was something rather abnormal in the gilded owl over the door. The owl was there as usual, being Mr. Burton's sign ; but Wraye had never before noticed that the eyes were glass, red glass, and to-night they glared at him like any stage owl in the Freischütz.   On examination it was plain enough that their brilliancy came from the reflection of the electric light on Madison Square. Wraye walked in and bought another of Flaubert's novels, and would have given the owl no further thought if he had not observed, on coming out, that one eye of the owl was closed and duly gilded, while all the red glare was concentrated in the other, which was wide open, and on his side of the bird.   Wraye had certainly been under the impression that both eyes were glass when he went in.

After all it was a matter of entire indifference to him whether his bookseller's gilded owl had one eye or two, winked at him or not; so, jumping into his carriage, he drove to his lodgings on Twentieth street. They were comfortable little rooms, near the Club ; and as he let himself in with his latchkey, he was glad to find that the lock had been treated with luminous paint.   On his dressing-table, among many notes and more bills, was a familiar billet with a dainty little crest, sealed in red wax.   Now, why the deuce does Mrs. de Monégo perfume her notes so? thought he, as he tore it open ; and the perfume was not so nice as usual either, but reminded him of his own cologne water in the train.   *Mrs. de Monégo will be happy,* etc.   *Mr. Wraye's presence,* etc., etc.   "Of course she will," thought Wraye ; " the question is whether I shall.   Halloa ! it's to-night ! "

Well, on the whole, by Jove ! Wraye thought he would go.   After all, and ten weeks in Tennessee, it was worth while to hear what was going on in the world, and see a Christian woman again. The last had been Mrs. Jenkins, and she was Methodist. Then Van Buskirk had probably been making no end of running while he was away. So Wraye went to the shelf in his wardrobe, and pulled down his new dress-suit, and his gibus hat, and his shirt, and his studs, and his ties, and then could not find his eye-glass, which had not been needed in the mountains. The dress-suit was clean, but it had been folded so long that there were deep creases in the trousers; and the camphor, or other preservative used by his valet, was disgustingly strong and pungent. However, Wraye got into it, and then had a carriage called and got into that, and was driven to the narrow but fashionable front of Mrs. de Monégo's Madison Avenue residence. And sure enough there was Van Buskirk, leaning close over the fair shoulder of his hostess, saying to her sweet nothings, but looking to her sober somethings with his eyes. Wraye made for them at once, Van Buskirk welcoming him with something that was not a grin nor yet a leer, and was still further complicated by an inward curse.

But the beauteous dame received him most graciously. *It was an age since she had seen him. What had he been up to this long time? No good, no doubt.* Van Buskirk grinned. *What did he say — raising the devil? Ha, ha, ha —* (what a silvery laugh had Mrs. de Monégo just here. Van Buskirk joined in awkwardly as if he had not clearly heard, and thought he was

being made a butt of)—*ha, ha, ha! And had he
succeeded?* "No," said Wraye (Van Buskirk got up
in disgust and clumsily removed himself, the lady
scarce recognizing his parting bow), "no—how
were that possible, the Lady Lilith away?"

Mr. Pillian Wraye could turn a very neat compliment
when he tried, and Mrs. de Monégo colored at one
of the two things left in life that gave her pleasure—
appreciation by a man of her personal beauty. Wraye
took advantage of the pause to look over at Van Buskirk. He was standing alone in a corner, scrunching
up his hat against his shirt-bosom, and his expression
by this time was simply diabolical. *Aha!* thought
Wraye, *the absent are not always in the wrong, my
friend, especially when they return from Tennessee.*
Wraye was very clever and satirical that night; few
of the older women escaped his lash, and none of the
pretty ones. A second time he delighted Mrs. de
Monégo, who was possibly the worst woman in the
room, but hated to think herself so. Not that any
one of them was very bad : we live in a virtuous
republic, and the devil himself is probably a very
average good sort of fellow to-day.

Wraye had meant to speak to a young girl in white
tulle whom he saw in the distance. But there was
a certain triumph in carrying off so fashionable a
woman as Mrs. de Monégo from so accomplished a
swell as Van Buskirk; and before Wraye had got
through relishing his victory, Van Buskirk had
stepped in and was talking to the young girl in white

tulle himself. Wraye hated to see this, somehow or other ; and the girl in white tulle looked at him a little sadly as he and Mrs. de Monégo passed her, and then blushed for having done it.

Well, it was all very splendid, and the exact tingle of snow-crystals was in the wine, and the canvas-backs were deliciously bloody ; but all things, save a few we haven't yet met with, must come to an end some time. Wraye found himself walking home with Van Buskirk and an uncommonly fine cigarette that his vanquished rival had given him. It was a snapping fine night, and as they passed the mansion of a railway duke lately created its windows were ablaze with light.

" Electricity," muttered Van Buskirk.

" The deuce it is ! " thought Wraye.

" Yes," said his friend. " Those wretched companies bring it round." Wraye was puzzled, and looked at Van Buskirk, wondering if he owned the gas company, or had taken a drop too much.

" As you say," Van Buskirk added, " that canvas-back was good. But come into the Club and take something. I feel like a boiled owl."

" Or a gilded one," suggested Wraye.

" Ha, ha, yes !— very good. Or a gilded owl ! Ho, ho ! Devilish good, by Jove ! My dear fellow, come into the Club and have a bottle of wine."

Wraye had not intended to be so extraordinarily funny, and he had meant to go home reasonably early—before two o'clock—and get up betimes in the morning for some work of the little work that he had in this world to do.

"It will do just as well to-morrow," Van Buskirk put in, "and it doesn't amount to much, anyway." Wraye secretly feared that it did not, indeed, amount to very much; and was hardly offended with Van Buskirk for telling him so.

"You can't do anything that way, old boy," he went on. "The fact is, the people have made up their minds what they want; and there's no use getting yourself disliked by setting up as a prophet." Wraye thought Van Buskirk talked devilish sensibly for a fellow that had taken so much to drink. "Since they want to go to the deuce, let 'em, confound 'em. Now," Van Buskirk concluded, with a wave of his hand, as they mounted the stone steps of the Club, "they can't get in here — what more do you want? There's plenty of fun in the world for you and them."

There were a few men still in the smoking-room when they entered. They all nodded to Van Buskirk, and one or two looked at Wraye. After all, despite his victory that evening, Wraye was not so prominent a man as Van Buskirk socially. This sort of reflection never passed through Wraye's mind without leaving a sting; and when Van Buskirk asked him if he would take something, he promptly answered that he would, although wine was certain to disagree with him taken late at night.

Van was really a very pleasant fellow. He sat down that night with Wraye and told him all the dear old talk that one hears nothing of in the mountains and is not murmured by the sea : talk that one misses in the woods, and can't get even in town save in just the right set, which makes so much the charm of it—how the Joneses were making their way in society, and the Smiths could not ; how Teddy Headstrong had made a scandalous marriage, and Sally Hart wanted to ; how Ethel Hartless was reported engaged to old Margin, and who was the last man Mrs. Malachyte Bowlder had taken up. Fashion, thought Wraye, is its own reward. Without it, if you are once in society, there is no further step. Was it not Pelham who called Fashion a subtler goddess that even nobility of birth ? There is nothing else which can really give you distinction among your peers ; it is the one merit which all the world can see and recognize. Van Buskirk had many little society schemes to submit to Wraye, and our hero gave them his earnest attention.

Another fellow joined them and told some very good stories. About the end of the first bottle of wine, thinking of his weeks on the mountain, Wraye's spirits suffered a slight reaction. He told Van Buskirk a *bon mot* he had made — that the peculiar gratification of being fashionable was to persuade both another fellow and yourself that you were better than he, when you both of you knew that you weren't. Van Buskirk didn't seem to think that this was very funny, and Wraye was a little piqued. '' Come and have a smoke, old man,'' said he ; '' light a weed." Wraye did so, and nearly choked himself with a sulphur match. "You should use parlor matches," said Van Buskirk, and he lit a fusee.

They went into the little smoking-room, where there is a weathercock over the fire-place, telling which way the wind is blowing outside. Van Buskirk was standing before the fire. Most men, when they stand before a fire, part their coat-tails and hold one in either hand; but Wraye noticed that Van Buskirk's coat-tails were sewed together behind, and wondered if it was the latest fashion. "Pretty little girl, that is," said Van Buskirk, speaking of the one in white tulle. "Saw you looking at her at the party. Pity she hasn't more style."

Wraye didn't quite like this way of speaking of her. Still, he said nothing; there was no use breaking this agreeable intimacy for a few words. "Now, Meg Moidore—ah, there's a girl!" Van Buskirk went on, smacking his lips. "Nothing countrified about her. Take something?"

Wraye was a little taken aback, and murmured something about the lateness of the hour.

"Nonsense," said the other. "Just beginning to be pleasant. Ring the bell, will you, old fellow?"

Wraye didn't quite like being ordered about so; still, it was pleasant to be called "old fellow." He touched the electric bell, which imparted a sharp prick to his forefinger, and noticed as he did so that the weathercock was spinning rapidly around the face of the dial, backward.

"Ah," said Van Buskirk, "it's all the electricity. Great night for electricity — I told you so. Where was I? Oh, yes. Well, the fact is, you see, it's all very well for women who've nothing better to look forward to until they *are* married — Waiter, a couple of hot whiskys, if you please." "And a cigar," added Wraye, as the waiter left the room. The bell rang again. "And two cigars," said Van Buskirk. "The fact is, you see —"

"Who the deuce rang the bell?" broke in Wraye.

"Why, I did," said Van Buskirk. "Don't interrupt so. Now, for you and me, you know, as men of the world, marriage is a mistake. When people thought it was a duty — halloa, here's the whisky." The waiter brought two little stone pitchers, steaming from their pewter tops, and a decanter. Van Buskirk poured out two glasses of the mixture.

"Cayenne pepper?" said he.

"No," said Wraye; and he clinked his glass with Van Buskirk's. As he approached it to his lips, the liquid suddenly hissed up into a blue flame.

"Great heavens!" cried Wraye, shoving his chair back, "what's that?"

"What's what?" growled Van Buskirk. "My dear boy, don't be so excited, and, above all, so profane. Now, if you were Miss Mary —"

"Who the devil mentioned her name?" cried Wraye, suddenly growing ill-tempered.

"Who the devil? Why, my dear boy, you know

you've been talking to me about it these three months. As for Mrs. de Monégo —"

" Curse Mrs. de Monégo ! "

" Be at ease about that, old chap ; it's all provided for.   But as for that little chit who's hardly in society —"

" I tell you I don't wish to hear any more of her, or you either ! " roared Wraye.

" Come, come, don't talk so loud ; you'll attract attention.   When you called upon me, politely and ceremoniously as the thing was done, you really couldn't expect a fellow like me to leave town in the middle of the season for a beastly, stupid hole up on a mountain without even so much as a summer hotel —"

" I call upon you ?   I never asked you to go with me," Wraye shouted, jumping up and upsetting the table.   Who are you ?   Who in hell—"

" Exactly," said Van Buskirk with a smile and a bow.   " Same man, old chap."   The room began to go round and round.   The odor of sulphur was suffocating.   Van Buskirk's pale face leered through the cigar-smoke with the same expression it had worn at Mrs. de Monégo's.   At the same time something sinuous and hairy protruded from Van Buskirk's coat-tails, wound itself around his glass, and carried the flaming mixture to his lips.

Exorciso te, bellowed our hero in terror, and he hurled the decanter of hot water at Van Buskirk's glowing eyes.   A shriek of demoniac laughter reverberated through the empty Club ; Van Buskirk dodged the decanter and vanished in a flame of fire through the floor.

Wraye sank senseless on a sofa. When he awoke, one of the Club servants was pulling him by the sleeve of his dress-coat. It was morning. He went home to dress and came back to the Club for breakfast. After coffee, he plucked up courage to ask an acquaintance if he had seen anything of Van Buskirk that morning.

" He sailed for Europe last night," was the reply. " Some of the boys gave him a supper down the harbor on a tug."

Wraye said no more.

After lunch and a bottle of Pommard, Wraye read an essay on *Visions* in a popular scientific monthly, and decided that it was all a dream.

Wraye still has his moments of approval for the True and the Beautiful, and is not without a feeling that he would like to do great and noble things.

Hitherto the only tangible result of his visit to Tennessee has been a large balance of income which, living on the mountain-top being inexpensive, now lies for investment at his banker's.

This will enable him to employ the labor of one additional third of an American citizen, at the current average price of $1.62 1-2 cents *per diem*.

March.

The Seven Lights of Asia: An Indo-European Episode.

AN ALLEGORY FOR EASTER.

IN Asia there is a certain range of mountains, composed of everlasting hills, and the highest and most durable of them is called Everest. The name of the range is Himalaya, which means cradle of peoples, and through it there runs an extraordinary and most noteworthy valley. You will find mention of it in no atlas; and Murray and Baedeker are still striving in vain to find some traveler who has been through it and can write a guide. There is, indeed, one old handbook, published centuries since; but many people think this of doubtful

accuracy, as it was originally printed in Greek and
other languages which are now dead.   These people
think that the world has progressed since then, and
clamor for a new edition; and some ambitious fellows
of the Geographical Society have even attempted to
produce one.   But they have hitherto failed to agree
upon the publisher, and are still at odds about the
color of the binding.

This valley begins at the mountain of Everest; it
is called Lheurequilest, and is swept (like most of the
valleys of the Himalaya) by the peculiar and devastat-
ing wind named llnyena.   There are some travelers
who profess to like this cold wind, and call it bracing;
but, all the same, it brings the water to their eyes
and they do not see very far.

No one has ever described the route by which you
reach this valley.   The peculiarity of the journey (if
it can be called a journey) is that you do not commonly go thither at all.   You find yourself there.
But often you are there several years before you find
yourself; and when you do, you rarely know yourself.   When you do that, you wish you had never
been born.   And there is also a peculiarity about the
place.   When you are away from it, you give it many
and various names; but, while you are in it, it is
always Lheurequilest.

Now the chronicles of Safiz, the Persian, upon
whose stories Zerdusht based the greatest part of his
writings, tell us that long ago — many lives of a dog-
star since — there arrived in this valley a rare and

wonderful traveler. He called the valley of Lheurequilest by another name — *Aei*. Learned pandits
differ as to the meaning of this word, some tracing
it back to a Greek root, while others see in it only an
interjection. Be that as it may, the voyager of whom
we speak never spoke of the place by any other name
than Aei. And when he first uttered this cry the
clocks all struck thirteen, and there came a sort of
chorus from the Devas in the clouds, while three
hundred Pratycka Buddhas, who were practicing their
religious exercises in a forest near by, immediately
rose into the air and went together to Benares. Here,
in this city, they began to exhibit their supernatural
powers, causing their bodies to ascend into space and
emit all sorts of brilliant appearances : thus, one after
another, they uttered a Gâtha, and, ending their term
of days, entered Nirvàna.

Meantime the traveler was looking about him. He
was very young for a man, and we may call his name
Smith, as being generic. He had forty teeth, and his
arms were very long, so that his long and tapering
fingers reached to the knee. High as was his instep,
his long hair was more yellow, and it curled around
the crown of his head from left to right. But what
of all was most remarkable about him was a strange
and beautiful white light, a radiance which seemed
to center in his brow, where a circlet of rare jewels
bound his head. Such was the magic of these stones
that each separate ray was blended in a glory like the
light of day ; and those old Hindus knew no better,

and could not see the separate stones that made it up.
But now, as every public school-girl may know, we
have pulled the light of day to pieces; and so this,
too, was but a spectral splendor, and the jewels com-
posing it are known to science.   They are common
stones enough — a deep blue sapphire and an aqua-
marine, an emerald, a topaz and an opal, a ruby and
an amethyst.   Doubtless it was mere chance that
the seven jewels were the seven colors of the rain-
bow; and you may buy any of them for money on
Broadway.

Hardly had Smith opened his blue eyes and rubbed
them, to find his whereabouts, when the blast made
him shiver; it was that Black Bise or Ilnyena, which
blows so endlessly in the narrow valley, like a dark
wind of the Trades.   He cast his eyes up, but only
to those gray clouds which learned pandits call the
veil of Maja.   He followed with his glance the clouds
to the eastward, hoping for some horizon that was
blue; but the high mountains that were behind him
shut it out.   He turned his glance to the west; but
at that end of the valley rose still higher mountains,
their summits lost in mist.   Then he looked down,
and saw a vast, motley crowd coming along the
beaten road, wrangling as they came; and as he bent
his head the deepest and most beautiful jewel of them
all fell into a muddy pool at his feet.   For a long
time he sought in the turbid water for the sapphire's
blue light; but the pool was stagnant and shallow,
and the surface dense with decaying leaves, and

continually stirred by the footsteps of the multitude. All in vain he looked for the precious stone, sorrowing as for a birthright he had lost; and when he gave up the search, it was to him as if he had forgotten God.

By this time he was surrounded by a motley crowd of men; and he saw that some were travelers like himself, and others were guides and porters. Among these latter many wore brass-plates, as being duly licensed, while others only showed him mountain staves. One old guide, whom they all called Papa Peter, had already a large party of tourists, who were going through under his guidance, personally conducted; and thick tourists' veils were bound about their eyes, lest the dust of the road should irritate them. These seemed rather quiet. Not so another licensed guide, a younger man, who was disputing with their leader, and had quite a company gathered about him too. Then there was another one yet, a loud-mouthed fellow, with banners and transparencies; and a great number of others who did not belong to the association of licensed guides at all, and offered cheaper rates. But it was said of these that they were mere porters, not passed guides, and that they had never really been over the mountain at all. Now, Smith was well determined to go through the valley and over the mountain at the end; but he could not choose among so many guides, so he decided to walk on alone for the present and join one of the parties later on. At this there was a great cry, and all the people set after him with sticks, so that he had to run for safety to a thick and lonely wood.

Here he walked for a long time alone ; but he was troubled at their treatment of him, and the light of his brow was not so clear since the sapphire had been lost, though he needed all the light he could get to make way through the lonely forest. Little light from the sky came into the wood, and he was fain still to turn to his fellow-travelers for assistance ; but their numbers gave them assurance, and they cried out at him and made grimaces because he was alone. Now and then he met another traveler wandering in the forest like himself ; but these were mostly moody fellows, and he still yearned for the companionship of the multitude. In this way, however, he struck up some friendship with a Frenchman and a wise German ; but the Frenchman, though a pleasant fellow, was a singularly bad walker ; and the German, though he walked well enough, would have nothing to do with the multitude or the direction in which they were going, but was always for stopping and trying to construct a balloon which would carry them from where they were straight up into the sky. Then there was an Englishman, who had a map ; but it was of the valley only, and all beyond was blank. And when Smith asked for a chart of the country outside of this map, the Englishman asked if he did not see from the map that there was nothing outside, and called him a fool.

Again Smith went back to the multitude and found that some of the loudest in speech had dropped behind, and the rest were tired and more kindly. Every one of them professed to be going his way, and to have the highest mountain in view. Some of them even claimed, by the aid of spy-glasses of transcendent power, to see over the mountains entirely ; but though they all said that they were anxious to help him, he did not get along very fast.   In fact, very few of them seemed to think that they were going anywhere in particular ; and all were more concerned about the rank and arrangement of the procession than with the progress that it made. Then one man was always for stopping in every pleasant place to pluck the berries ; another seemed to be a geologist, and kept stopping to pick up any shining stone he saw in the earth ; a third was continually making sketches ; and a fourth kept beating all his neighbors with a stick, to make them go his way.

There were several bands for the march, but none of them played the same tune ; and many of the wayfarers had picked up sticks and stones, feathers or wreaths, tiaras and coronets, on which they greatly plumed themselves, and which made them look like a German picnic. Among them there was one gentlemanlike person, with an iron weapon, which he called his sword of honour.   At first Smith was rather attracted by him ; most of the other wayfarers were continually ascending little

foothills, where they would stop the whole company
to look at them, and see how high they were, each
one claiming that his hillock was the true summit
of the mountain, that he would go no further, and,
at all events, that he was higher up than the rest;
but among all these the traveler with the sword
walked on with a sort of humble disdain. Smith
noticed with despair that his own aqua-marine was
growing looser and looser, and he finally gave it to
his comrade for safe-keeping; but no sooner had he
fairly got the jewel than he ran eagerly away with it,
and, crossing an impassable stream, destroyed the
bridge behind him.

At this our poor traveler lost faith in all his fellow-
pilgrims. It seemed to him that each one was satisfied if he could only persuade the others that he was
a little further on than they, and none of them cared
much about reaching their destination. For a long
time he sat by the stream's bank with his head bowed
down, looking at the circlet from which the two first
jewels were gone, having no faith in man and no
certainty of God. He had to make a long *détour* to
get around the water, and with this loss of light the
path seemed harder than ever to find; but he picked
up the sword that the robber had dropped, and with
it hewed his way through the wilderness.

Still, the sword was only meant for defense, and
did little service as a staff on the long and weary
way. And now the emerald, too, was growing dull,
and seemed to give less light. He had been hoping

that the path would ascend; but it always went down and down, lower and lower into the heart of the valley. All through the day there had been little rills that crossed the path and seemed to ripple with sweet music from some higher place; but even these grew silent, as they fell into the central plain. Still many noonday hours he struggled on, hoping; and the weary path stretched endless leagues away, and the fresh light of the emerald was nearly gone. At last the way lost itself in a swamp, where he fell exhausted, hedged in by the crawling vines and sickened by the fat mists exhaling from the lower pools. A ghastly place it was; he alone seemed to be alive; but all about the pools lay myriads of figures, bodies of former pilgrims, dead or numbed. Here he lost all hope; and, finding one poor girl whose heart was faintly beating, gave her the emerald. But then it seemed to him that he saw a faint light forward, and heard a broken bar of some far-distant song; so rising once more, he plodded on, leaving hope with her.

It was well he did this; for soon he came to a grove of trees and flowers, alive with singing birds, filled through and through with such a golden light that it seemed as if it must come from the sky. Was this the light that he had seen below, he wondered. After a moment's rest, he ran back to find the girl to whom he had given the emerald. She wore it in her bosom, and in her possession the jewel still seemed bright. He took her in his arms, and bore her to the grove;

and then ran back again and again, to show to other
pilgrims the road thither. Smiling, the girl encour-
aged him to do this; and many pilgrims thus were
saved and went their way. And as he staid there, so
laboring, in the cool of the early afternoon, it seemed
to him that they were perfectly happy; and he gave
her the glorious golden topaz for a ring. Already he
could see, as he looked back upon his early journeying, though slowly, through the plain, the path had
risen; and all the way behind was lower land. But
when he returned, after one of his journeys of assistance, they told him that the young girl had gone
further on. His glorious golden topaz was still with
her, and it seemed to him that earthly happiness had
gone from him with this. And of the seven jewels
heaven gave him, this was the fourth that he had
given to his fellow-men. He buckled on his sword,
and followed in the footsteps of his lost companion.

They say that more than midway through the valley
is a lovely garden, embowered on the brow of a hill.
High trees grow about it, and shut it in from the
mountains and shield it from the wind of Ilnyena;
and all the flowers of the earth grow there. • Here are
fountains that plash, and orchestras that make sweet
music; and from the colonnades and pavilions you
get fair views and vistas, flower-framed — the fairest
views that are to be had of the valley of Lheurequilest. No one knows who first laid out this garden, but all the writers agree that it exists. Hither,
at last, our traveler came; and here seemed to be the

fountains of the rills that spread abroad through the valley and had so refreshed him on the march. Here, too, was the music and all the singing of which he had heard the echo or the faint refrain. All that was beautiful in sight or sound was here. He also learned a song ; and, joining the others, sought with what voice he could to swell the choral that floated downward to the plain. The chorister was invisible ; but the Arabic version of this story tells us that it is the angel Israfel.

Some old men still lingered here, laureled and embayed, poets and artists, beauty-makers to the world ; and our traveler might also have staid but that he noticed that his keen sword was growing tarnished by the rich, sweet air. Then he watched these older men, and marked that they too went onward, one by one. I have said that all that was beautiful in sight or sound was here ; and now he saw that each of these old men had a flashing opal, like his own, which he drew from his wrinkled brow and burned before departing. So he took his own and tried it in the fire ; its genius flashed out into a radiant blaze that must have shown far down through the wilderness in the valley ; and, indeed, there was a sort of after-glow which was reflected far off from cliff to cliff, like an echo of enduring sound. Now he saw what had been the birth of the strange far-off lights that had cheered him upward so often on the way. (And here the Persian legend has a pretty story that the light of our wayfarer's burning opal still lingers in the valley, like the colors in the clouds when the sun has gone.)

So at last he left the garden, and went forward on his way, and came out on the bleak side of the mountain, so high that all the valley seemed faint and far to him, like the memory of a dream.   The wind was still chilly, and the place dark with evening, and only the grave ruby and the amethyst remained to light his way.   Other pilgrims seemed to think that he was wise, and came to him with queries.; but the light of the ruby was but a narrow sphere, and all the world beyond was lost in the night.   He was in the upper gorges of the mountain ; but the crown still seemed far off.   He grew cold and weary ; even the ruby seemed to fail him ; he dropped it from his hand, caring little for the wisdom of the world.   Strange purple flashes came through the cloud.   Still grasping the purple amethyst, he sank upon the snow.   A strange voice spoke in his ears; he tried to answer, saying who he was, whence he came, whither he was going ; but the one poor word that his lips could utter the jewel gave him—love.

It was the last of the Seven Lights to leave him ; but, as he spoke, the wind seemed to buoy him forward, and he reached the utmost ridge, and the purple jewel flashed out and melted in the purple sky.   For there beyond him (so runs one version of the Persian story)—there beyond him was the open world and the cloudless west, and all around the mountains lay the clear horizon he had sought at first.   Backward, the valley was still dark, and the mists were floating low. The Seven Lights were gone.

But in the dark valley he saw the multitude, with faces all upturned ; and lo ! in the look of each there lingered some far light, some faint reflection of some light that he had early lost. Some looked up to him with eyes of hope, and pious lips of faith, and lights of genius, happiness, and human love. And now he looked again ; and far behind the Eastern mountain was the light of God. Its radiance was of the sapphire he had lost in the beginning. The faces of the multitude were turned away ; they could not see it ; but, as he stood there, far above them, he saw it falling down before them on the path.

April.

A First Love-Letter.

FOR THE UNCERTAIN GLORY OF AN APRIL DAY.

IT was a warm day in the bush. There was no wind ; and the atmosphere was in successive layers, superposed, shimmering with the heat. The canvas-topped carts of the detachment were clumped to-gether in a circle. On three sides the level, gray-green plain, broken in its sandy sameness only by an occasional clump of sage-bush or of prickly pear, stretched as far as one could see. On the fourth side was a low, apparently insignificant, but wholly impenetrable African thicket of indefinite extent. Trackless, tan-gled, arid, it was fit only to be the lurking-place of hyenas and snakes, or Zulus. How much of a lurking-place it might be for the latter was a present and interesting question. Most of the company in the little camp were thinking of it. Captain Philip Haughton, in his private and particular tent, had ceased thinking about it.

There are many rapid transitions in modern life,—
changes of scene and *décor*,—but probably even
Americans know few extremes more startling than
Piccadilly and Zululand.   As much as the Captain's
somewhat inactive mind was occupied with anything,
it was busied with this reflection.   It did not particularly surprise, much less excite him, this change.
The young stoic of Belgravia probably takes—he
certainly affects to take—about the same interest in
such changes as he does in those of scenery in a
theatre ; they are sometimes amusing; but more likely
to be bores.   However, there was uncommonly little
affectation in Captain Phil's case.   He had no reason
whatever to regret leaving Piccadilly.   It was after
the season ; and at such times St. James's street was
a desert hardly more frequented, and infinitely less
amusing, than South Africa.   The only people you
saw at the clubs were men you would avoid even in
South Africa.   The regular round of country visits
had begun ; but as there was only one person whom
Haughton particularly desired to meet, and she was,
at the same time, one whom it was very important
he should not meet,—in brief, he did not much
regret the loss of his various weeks in the shires.
As for shooting, the partridges were mostly drowned,
and black game scarce, he was told.   And the Zulus
were perhaps a more exciting and better preserved
black game than either.   " By Jove ! I should think
so," he thought, lazily, in applause of his own
epigram.   " Battues are nothing to it."   The Captain was always ready to laugh at little or nothing.

And he now smiled again, sweetly, as he reflected more precisely upon the position in which he found himself.

He was sitting upon a shawl, which he had doubled up on the sand. The shawl was in front of a tent; and the tent was in a sort of arena, surrounded by a circle of white-covered carts, their rear and open ends facing inside — some of them still filled with stores, others serving as temporary shelter. Close outside, and around them all, was a rampart of wattled underbrush. Between each two was a practicable loophole, through which was thrust a rifle; beside each rifle rested the owner, in the enjoyment of a short clay pipe. Outside, at a distance of a few hundred yards, was a circlet of pacing sentries, who marched as if they were trying to pretend it was all an unusually warm review in the Park, knowing their commanding officer liked style, in South Africa or elsewhere. They were fond of their commanding officer. Inside again, at the shady end of the arena (while there was a shady end), a number of long-horned, gaunt cattle were picketed ; near them, the few remaining horses of the command.

Behind the Captain, in the interior of the tent, stood the Captain's servant, engaged in polishing the tops of the Captain's boots. This he did with much attention and solicitude. He knew, with all the rest of the little command, — with the corporals, the lieutenants, the buglers, and almost the poor, jaded horses themselves, — that the Captain and his company were in a nasty mess. And in common with

the rest of them, he sometimes took the liberty of
wondering how they were to get out of it ; that is,
supposing that they were to get out of it.

Captain Haughton, however, had got away beyond
that question.   It was an idle habit of his to give up
problems too difficult for immediate solution.   Besides, his orders left him positively no option.   He
was to repair to a certain position, and hold it until
the main body came up, keeping the Zulus in check.
It had been supposed that the Zulus to be kept in
check numbered only a thousand or so ; but the
orders applied equally well to the checking of any
amount of them.   As his servant gave the last careful rub to the upper rim of his boots, the Captain
was, in fact, thinking not at all of the Zulus, but of
the last ball he had gone to in London.   He remembered particularly the heat of the conservatory.   The
very scents and dead sweetness of the place seemed
to be still in his nostrils.   He could see it now—the
black coats and white shoulders, the gleam of diamonds against the shiny background of green leaves.
"Like the eyes of snakes in a Zulu thicket," thought
the Captain ; "only not so frank in their malice,"
he added, gloomily. Haughton was a heavy, straight-
forward fellow by nature ; and perhaps his attempts
at cynicism were clumsy.

It was hotter than ever, and there was a drowsy
noise of insects in the air.   The Captain's servant
came forward just then with the Captain's boots.
He hesitated a moment, and looked at his master, the

boots in one hand. He was uneasy; he had rarely seen Captain Philip so quiet.

"Any orders, sir?" touching his hat.

"No—or, stop—yes," said the Captain. "Ask private Fairlie to come to me."

Saying which, the Captain leaned back as if overcome with the exertion of speaking, drew an embroidered tobacco-pouch from his pocket, and rolled a cigarette. As he looked at the tobacco-pouch, he became conscious of a tingling sensation in the bridge of his nose, which, having been very much sunburned, had begun to peel. This tobacco-pouch bore the initials *A. M.—P. H.*, and was a favorite trinket of his. Out of it, it had been his custom (being always a lazy man) to tease .his fair friends into rolling cigarettes with their own white fingers.

"I am a damned fool," he remarked, with more emphasis than the occasion seemed to require. It was perfectly natural that his sunburned nose should tingle. Lighting his cigarette, he puffed a moment vigorously; but it was badly made, and the tobacco soon escaped from a seam at the side. Before he had time to roll another, a stout, blue-eyed countryman in the garb of a soldier stood before him; and the Captain became aware that private Fairlie had saluted him, and was looking at him with an expression of unmistakable affection in his simple countenance.

"Private Fairlie?"

"Yes, your honor," said Fairlie, with another salute.

"You are the man whose horse was shot under him, and who rode behind me into camp from the skirmish yesterday?"

"Oh, your honor—" began Fairlie, with yet another salute; but this attempt at military discipline did not conceal a most undoubted blubber.

"There, there!" said the Captain, "enough of that. You were nearly senseless when I picked you up, and you said something about Kate. If I mistake not, that name, which I take to be feminine, was several times repeated during our ride. Now you will overlook my curiosity, but I should really like very much to know. Who is Kate?"

"Kate, your honor? Why, Kate—Kate? I don't mind telling your honor—she—your honor knows, she lives near father's farm—and she said as how she'd—leastwise, she wouldn't *then*, your honor—but she said as how she'd have me if so be as I comes back from the wars alive; and you see, your honor, when I got under that there horse, sir, it come kind of natural to think of her, and—"

"Private Fairlie, you're a fool."

"Yes, your honor."

The conversation ended, as it had begun, with a salute. The Captain rubbed his nose with his handkerchief, which caused the upper part of that organ to tingle as before. Fairlie, having no handkerchief, scraped the sand with the inner edge of his right boot.

The heat was really terrific, and both men were daz-
zled with the glare of the white tent.   There was a
smell of dust and horses ; the camp was so still that
the cattle could be heard striking the earth at the opposite end of the arena.   The Captain rose and looked
through the end of his tent between two of the carts.
There was a double force of sentries on duty, and
they were intently watching the low edge of bush
that rimmed the plain.   There was nothing to show
that the bush was occupied.   He returned to Fairlie.

" Private Fairlie, do you suppose Kate would care
if you lost your precious skin ? "   The Captain spoke
gruffly.   Fairlie stared at him stupidly.   At first he
seemed disposed to tears again.   Finally he grinned.

" Private Fairlie," said the Captain, more quietly,
" I wish you to carry some dispatches back to Colonel
Haddon at the general headquarters.   You will take
my horse, and start at dusk.   He will carry you over
the sixty miles before dawn.   Of course, you must
escape unseen.   There is no moon, and you must be
within call of the sentries at headquarters before day-
break.   You will deliver the dispatches to Colonel
Haddon himself.   It is a chance if you get there with
the dispatches ; but if you do, there will be among
them a letter asking for a furlough for yourself.
When you have got it, you will return to England,
and take a letter I shall give you to the person to
whom it is addressed.   Mind, you must insist on
putting it into her own hands."   Fairlie saluted.
" When you have done this, you will go back to

Derbyshire, and I strongly advise you to stay there. I will give you money to purchase your discharge. You understand?"

Private Fairlie was a stupid man; but, after some moments' hesitation, he replied, huskily, "Yes, your honor."

"Good, my man. You can go."

Fairlie touched his hat mechanically, and turned away. He had hardly got beyond the door of the tent when he turned, rushed back, grasped the Captain's hand, and then, with a *"Beg pardon, sir,"* strode off to his mess. Meantime the Captain, it being an hour before sunset, closed the curtain of his tent and wrote two letters. The first was brief, and has been printed in army reports and in the newspapers as the last authentic report from his command:

"CAMP DERBYSHIRE, May 20, 1879.

"SIR: I have the honor to report a large force of Zulus in the front, estimated at over four thousand. It will be impossible for us to sustain a general attack. It therefore seems advisable that we should be reënforced at the earliest possible date, or the position we now hold reoccupied with much greater force. I have the honor to be,

"Your most obedient servant,

PHILIP HAUGHTON, Captain.

"Lieut.-Col. Haddon, C. B."

The second was longer, and has never been printed:

"To MISS ALICE MANNERS,

Axe-edge Moor, Derbyshire, England.

"I love you, Alice, and have always loved you. I have sometimes thought you knew it. If you did not know it, I write to tell you; if you did, to forgive you.

" O my darling ! you will pardon my telling you this now, will you not ? You have given me no right to send you a love-letter, dearest ; but this is one; yet do not be angry until you have read it all. Let me think, now, that perhaps you love me now, and now only ; and that I would kiss you if you were here. My love — darling, do not throw the letter down. I wanted to tell you that I loved you — how much, you will never know ; but you might have learned from others that I loved you, and I wanted to tell you myself before I died.

" I am here at an outpost in Africa, with half a company. The orders are to hold our camp at all hazard, and we shall certainly be attacked before dawn. If I thought there was any hope of our escaping, I should not write to you thus ; but you will pardon me, dear, for we cannot retreat, and there is no chance of defense or reënforcement. Indeed there is not.

" My men all know it, too ; but they are very quiet. They are brave fellows, and I think they like me. Perhaps it is wrong in me to send one of them away to carry this letter to you ; but he is a Derbyshire man, and was crying to-day over his sweetheart, and I could not help it. I wanted him to get home to her ; and one less to be killed here makes little difference. I should like you to help him a little when he gets to England.

" I hope that you are very happy. You must forgive me for telling you. You will not think it wrong for me to write so — now ? "

" Good-bye, dear Alice.

" PHILIP HAUGHTON."

It was some months after the date of this letter that the guests at Carysbridge Hall, in Derbyshire, were awaiting dinner. It is a nuisance, waiting for dinner ; particularly when you are standing before the fire, as was Major Brandyball, and supporting a portly person in patent-leather pumps a trifle small. Dinner was a formal affair at Carysbridge. There were many guests for the pheasant shooting, and Sir

John was entertaining largely in honor of his young wife. But a man had come just before dinner, and had insisted on seeing Lady Cary personally ; and she had now been gone nearly half an hour.

"I wonder who it can be?" said the Countess Dowager to Brandyball. The Countess Dowager liked to know everything ; that is, everything about her friends. "The servant said the man seemed to be a soldier."

"I think," said the Major, "I think Lady Cary used to have some friends in the army — when she was Miss Manners."

Further conversation was checked by Lady Cary's return. She was a beautiful woman, Sir John's wife ; and she never looked better than on that night. The Major noticed that she held a letter crumpled in one hand ; and her haste had given her a heightened color. She must have been gone over half an hour.

"Forgive me for keeping you all so long," she said, with her sweet smile. "Lord Arthur, will you take the Countess Dowager in to dinner?"

May.

" Bill Shelby."

BEING THE STORY OF A CERTAIN MAY MORNING IN
EASTERN TENNESSEE.

NEVER met Bill Shelby but once, and then he gave me a silver half of a dollar. The manner of it was thus. My father's house (I don't mean the present one, which my uncle built; that is wooden and one-storied, and is but a poor affair, little better than a log cabin) — my father's old house was built of brick shortly after the Revolution, and was considered, at the time and since, to reflect much credit on the county. There were not many brick houses in the county even then (for the county has not grown much since); and this one of ours stood in the middle of Laurel Cove, and had five windows in front, with a door in the middle, a high-pitched roof, and a big chimney outside either end. The front door

opened into a great hall, with the biggest fire-place
of all at the back; and it was said of the staircase and
railing that it had been brought from Norfolk.   Not
that my grandfather was rich, but he had made many
friends during the war, and had served well up to
Yorktown; and when his duties were over, and the
Britishers had got their deserts, he came home to
settle and get married, and then he brought his wife
with him out there.   And among his friends were
some of those rich Norfolk merchants, with ships
coming almost every month from the old country;
and they made him a present of the carved staircase
and some hangings for the walls.   These hangings
were the wonder of the county for a long time.

Stair, or Starr, was my grandfather's name.   Starr
he used to pronounce it, and Starr my father spelled
it.   My grandfather was born in Maryland, and I
believe we are of a good family.   I have heard it said
that we used to be Romanists, but of course we
never talked much about that; we were all good
Presbyterians by the time I was raised.   When my
grandfather first came out from Maryland, he put
about all he had into this brick house, feeling he
must do proper honor to the carved staircase, and
start the family well under the Republic.   But after
this, he lived mostly by hunting.   There isn't much
farming in our end of the State, so all my uncles
struck out for themselves; and only my father, who
was the youngest of the family, staid at home, and
he took to surgery.   Dr. Starr he was called, and it

was said of him that he never lost a patient bitten by
a rattler or taken with the fall sickness, provided he
got to him in time. This was about all the sickness
we used to have up in our part of the country ; we
didn't call the ague sickness. My father used to say
the fall sickness came from the cows. I don't know
how that is ; possibly they eat something. It was
my father built the mill. He was the most considerable man in that part of the country, and a justice of
the peace ; so the neighbors used to bring their grist
to him to be ground, and their daughters to him to
be married, and would send for him such other times
as they were sick or got into trouble.

I don't remember all these things very well : you
see, I left there, after that meeting with Bill Shelby,
and came North ; but I remember the old house, and
how it stood in a pretty valley. I am sure the valley
was pretty. It was a bright green meadow, soft
and level, like a park set in the mountains ; and in
the spring these mountains flushed rosy as the dawn
with the blossoms of the rhododendron and the
mountain-laurel. The meadow was dotted with
our barns, and cow-sheds, and milk-cooling houses,
and little benches of bee-hives. The upper end was
dry, with good English grass for cows ; and down
below, near the ford, it used to sparkle on sunny
days, where the water spread out among the grasses.
The house stood close up to the bridle-path, so that
travelers might be seen and asked to enter. Travelers
did not often pass my father's house without tasting

his apple-jack ; and along by the side of the house ran the brook in a little artificial channel flagged with stone, and then it made an elbow and splashed over the mill-wheel overshot. Boys love to play about a mill, and I used to beg my father to let me pull down the slide to turn the water on the wheel when a neighbor came to grind his corn. When the mill was not in use, the great wheel stood still and glistened, wet and mossy, dripping in the flume, and the water ran to waste beneath it and spread out through the meadow. Since then I have never seen so green a meadow as was this. But I suppose the wheel is now dry like punk, and rotting in the stones for want of use.

This little stream is Laurel Run ; further down it is called Rock Creek, and Rock Creek runs into Limestone Creek, and that into Nolichucky, and Nolichucky and the Holston make the Tennessee. There are many little villages like this of ours. They call them coves in Eastern Tennessee ; and Shining Cove, just below us, is on the main road north, and has something to do with my story. This, too, is a pleasant little valley, quite shut in by the mountains ; so that the wet meadows make a mist in the air, and the sun hangs in the centre, silvery and near, as if he were a lamp set in the sky for that particular place, and had nothing to do in the rest of the world. Perhaps this is why they call it Shining Cove. The road through it is but a bridle-path, lost among the dense green rhododendrons, with not purpose enough in its direction to stay on one side of the stream. It fords the creek a dozen times in a mile, but such as it is, it is the only highway to be found for twenty miles or more between the two States. For we are Tennesseeans, Washington county men,—Unicoi county they call it now, for a reason you will see later on,—but the State line runs over the Unaka mountains, the great ridge just behind us, and Jinkins's, the next house, is in Carolina.

You men in the North don't know what the war meant to us ; indeed, I doubt you hard heard of us at all while the fighting was going on. You see, ours was only a guerilla warfare, and East Tennessee was not considered worth a great campaign. No pitched battles were fought up in the mountains about us. But we thought very much of our friends in Boston and Cincinnati and other Northern cities, if they knew little of us. I cannot say that we were any great abolitionists down our way ; not that we had many slaves, but most of the families had one or two old negroes in the household who had, perhaps, they or their fathers, been brought over from Virginia. I understand, now, that the war was fought by the abolitionists, and that the praise is due to a few great orators and philanthropists who stayed at home to inspire the nation with their eloquence, and bought the freedom of the negroes with the lives of half a million fellow-citizens. But we did not know it then ; we had not heard much of this, and we had too few slaves, and were too rude and far away, to realize the harm that slavery was doing. The first that any of us knew, my father came home from the county town one day, and said that news had come up from Knoxville the week before that the South Carolinians had been firing on the flag at Charleston, and were breaking up the Union. Now it was nigh on to eighty years that my grandfather had come back from Yorktown with the first American flag that had been seen west of our mountains; and we still had this flag, with the thirteen stars in it, though my grandfather was gone, having died a few years before, by the Lord's mercy, as I now see.

My father brought down this flag from its place of honor on the wall of the best room, and we looked at it that evening, and the neighbors came in. There was a star in the flag for South Carolina, but none was there for Tennessee. But we all felt that old Tennessee was there just the same : more shame for South Carolina if it was she that left to give her room. I don't remember that anything was said about the negroes that night, or even about State rights, of which I have heard so much since. The simple fact was that that was our flag. I believe, if my grandfather had been there, he would have started off with his old buff and blue coat, just as if it were the first year after Yorktown instead of the eightieth. I know that was what my father did, and most of the neighbors went with him. Off he went to the North the very next morning, and left me alone with my mother. He kissed my mother and me and told us

that he would come back soon with the Union
soldiers ; so we kept the Union flag and waited.

But the year passed, and another year came and
went, and the Union soldiers did not come. And all
our men were away—away in the Union army. Perhaps you did not know this in the North. I dare say,
though, that they knew it at Washington, and it was
wrong for them to leave us so. You shall not make
me go back of that. All our mountain counties were
left to the women and children, as well in North
Carolina and Northern Georgia as in Tennessee ; and
the women raised the corn and tended the cows and
bees, and I turned the mill to my heart's content,
small as I was. I suppose you never heard of Carter
county and Washington, Watauga, Mitchell, and
Ashe ? I suppose you think North Carolina was a
rebel State ?   There were 2000 voters in Carter, by
the government count ; but more than 2000 Carter
county men and boys were in the Union armies.
And as for us of Union,—it was called Unicoi, after
the war, from Union and Unaka,—I believe there was
hardly a man, young or old, fighting on the side of
the rebels, or even hidden at home. The crops had
to grow themselves mostly. I won't say our men
were better soldiers than those of the North, who
came down from their mills and workshops ; but we
were used to hunting and riding (I never saw the
Northern man that could sit a horse), and better knew
the enemies we were fighting with. It might have
gone hard with New-York and the moneyed places,

which had their theatres and their tea and coffee through the war, without those three hundred thousand clever rifles from the South. No, I do not believe you knew this in the East; but, I have heard tell, the Government knew it, only it was not thought strategic to send away soldiers to relieve us Union people in the South. It was not a vulnerable point of the rebels; and the Government was trying more to injure its enemies than to save its friends. There were three hundred thousand Southern men in the Northern armies, but the Washington authorities could not spare any even of them for East Tennessee. They were needed on the Peninsula, about New Orleans, at Manassas. Lincoln had heard of us, I know, and wanted to get to us; but Lincoln had not been trained at West Point, and there were simpler words that he understood better than strategy.

So the Southern highlands suffered for their loyalty, while the Government left them to their fate. But we were far up in the mountains, and no one thought the rebels would ever get to us; and that first summer after my father left, we heard nothing of the war, but only the hum of the bees in the meadow, just as usual, and the plashing of the water on the wheel. News came up, from down Knoxville way, again, that the rebels were getting the better of the fight, and the Union armies were drawn further and further away, and my mother used to read her letters and cry; but I played about the mill, as usual, and wondered what it all meant. I had never heard any

cannon, and would have given anything to see some
soldiers. I used to look at the old print of the sur-
render of Cornwallis, in the parlor ; and I think I fancied that Cornwallis and his soldiers had come back
again, for I asked my mother once if it was them
that father was fighting with. I was only twelve
years old ; and so it happened that I do not remember very much, until the morning that I met Bill
Shelby. But I know my mother used to make me
say my prayers for father every night, and she would
try to join in them and hide her tears.

It was in the spring of the third year I met Bill
Shelby. We were all happy then, because my father had
got a furlough for a week, and he had been staying at
home with us, and bidding us to hope and have faith in
the end. I did not know it then, but I see now that
he must have come home secretly, for he wore no uniform, and stayed in the house most of the time, only
seeing men who came to see him. I suppose he was
recruiting, and my Uncle Albert had been with us
too. He lived in North Carolina ; and one morning
at dawn he rode up to the door with some twenty
men, stout fellows all, going North. North Carolina
men they were — Tarheelers, you call them ; only there
is no turpentine up in our mountains, nor any of the
kind of men you call Tarheelers. And I remember,
the morning that they came, my father told me I might
play about the mill all I liked, but I was not to leave
it, and if any man passed by I was not to tell him
that we had any one with us ; for there were rebel

spies about by this time, and they knew my father
was a Union man, and many houses had been burned
down on Holston and the French Broad, though the
rebels had never come up to our little place.

Well, all these men, with Uncle Albert, came into
our house in the early morning ; for they had come
over the mountain from Carolina in the night, and
were on their way North to join the Union armies.
They knew that they could stop for a hiding-place in
pretty much every house in our part of the country ;
but it was not safe to travel down in the valley by
daylight ; and they were waiting in our house till the
evening before they started off again. I don't suppose (except at weddings or funerals) there had been
so many men in our hall since the old carved staircase
had been brought from Norfolk after the war, and I
remember my father told them the story of this as
they sat about the great log fire drinking apple-jack ;
and the old flag with its thirteen stars was brought
down and lay across the table, and they fell to, admir-
ing it, for they had not seen the like in three years.

Our great hall used to have the fire-place on the
further side, filling up all that end of the room, and
the famous staircase ran up as you entered ; and
around the chimney-piece were all the guns and rifles
the family had ever owned, good or bad, hung on
antlers and bear's claws, and the flat stones of the
floor were covered with skins ; and my father had
been reading the Bible and morning prayers longer
than usual, for it was a Sunday, and there the men

were, sitting about the fire. Now a big log fire is all
very well in the early dawn, even of a May morning,— in our country wood is rubbish ; and on
that day, I remember, the highest forests of the
mountains were all silvered with the frozen fog ;
and a beautiful thing is this frozen fog in the early
sunrise, especially with the rich pink glow of the
flowering laurel down below,— but as the sun came
higher and shone down to us in the valley, it grew
very warm ; and after smoking many dozen corn-
cob pipes, and telling all the stories they knew, and
how the war was going on, most of the men scattered about in various places and went to sleep
—some in the hall, some in the bedrooms, and
some even in the barn, for they had been up
all night, coming over the mountains from Carolina. It was then my father told me I might go
out and play around the mill. And I left him sitting with my mother, she no longer now in tears.

It was a long time since the mill had done any
grinding, and already the wheel was getting a little
mossy and soft with the rot. I turned on the brook
once or twice over the wheel, pushing the slide well
out, just to see how the fall would go, and to keep
the lilies in the water-way from drooping (and it was
well I had the habit of this, for these lilies and long
grasses saved a man's life, as you shall see), and then
I sat looking across the valley, which was so sweet,
just then, with the May morning. The frozen fog
had been sunned off the mountains long before this,

but the rosy glow of the laurel was deeper and more rich than ever.   I was looking down the road toward Tennessee; 1 believe they had a man as watchman on the other side of the house, the Carolina side; but no one expected any danger from the North, and one good night's ride would take my uncle and his friends well. on, almost into Western Virginia, where they would be safe.

I was growing sleepy with the first feeling of the summer, and my eyes blinked once or twice; and when 1 opened them a horseman stood beside me, with heavy spurs, a slouch hat, a rifle, and an old blanket and strap overcoat, of a kind the rebels often used; and as I looked down the road 1 saw a long file of cavalry just splashing through our brook in the ford at the foot of the cow-pasture.   1 looked at him and at them; and as 1 looked, he swung himself off his horse and stood beside me.

"Now, sonny," said he, "don't say a word except what I ask you. Is this house Dr. Starr's?"   He was a great big fellow, with a face terribly sunburned and a bushy beard, looking like my Uncle Albert; and he spoke hurriedly, and kept glancing down the road, where the other mounted men were coming.

"Yes," said I; "Dr. Starr is my father. Do you know my father?   Shall 1 fetch him?"   1 suppose I ought not to have said this; but, you see, 1 did not know.

The man seemed almost sorry at my answer, and said, "No," quickly. Then he looked down to the ford again, where the others were coming slowly, on the walk. "No, don't fetch him, my boy," said he. "Is — is there any other men with him?"

"My Uncle Albert is in the house," I answered. "And — but father said I must not tell. What is your name? Do you know my father?" You see, I thought everybody knew my father; and I never took him for a rebel. I thought of the rebels as being far off — with Cornwallis at Yorktown.

"No," said he, "I do not know your father; always remember that, my boy. And my name — my name is Shelby — Bill Shelby." And somehow, even then, I felt that Bill Shelby was not his real name. "Now, sonny," he went on, "I want you to come with me and show me the chickens. I like little boys; and I've got one at home just like you." So saying, he swung me up on his great shoulders, and strode off in the direction of the furthest cow-house. I remembered telling him that this was not the one where the chickens were kept; but he gave no heed to me, and when he got to the cow-house, he opened the door, carefully closed it again, and tossed me up on the hay-mow, no higher than his head. Then he got up himself, and putting me astride of his great muddy boot, he rode me up and down like a baby, and began talking to me.

"Now, little boy," he said, "I can't stay with you very long; but you stay here until it is dark, and don't you move on any account. Is there many of you at home?"

I told him we were all of us there — there with father and mother.

" Is your mother there, too?" said the big man, and I said, " Yes," and he sighed. I was about to talk to him of my mother, for I always liked to talk of her, when a crash of musketry made me jump and cry out ; but he put his broad hand across my mouth and held me in a grip like a vise. " That's nothing," he whispered to me hastily ; " they're firing at a mark — at turkeys. Don't you stir from here till sundown. Promise me that." And here he pulled out a strange-looking wallet from his gray flannel shirt ; in it was a euchre-deck of playing-cards, and a few dirty bank-notes, and some papers, all mixed well and sprinkled through and through with grains of smoking tobacco ; and way down from the bottom he pulled out a real silver half dollar — the only one there was. " Now, sonny, you stay here quiet till dark, and this is all your'n," and he pressed the coin into my hand. " Don't you mind anything you hear : if you come out afore sundown, I'll take that dollar back." I had never seen so much money before ; and while I was looking at it Bill Shelby slipped out and closed the door of the barn behind him, and I thought of running to show my half dollar to mother ; but another noise (or perhaps the memory of what I had promised to Bill Shelby) made me hold back.

While all this was happening, the rebels rode up to the door of our house. It seems that they had heard

of my uncle and his men, and had ridden around
them to cut them off; and so came back upon us by
the northern road. And when they got to the front
door, their leader, Major — well, we will call him
Whichehalse; it sounds better — Major Whichehalse,
he knocked on the door with the pommel of his
sword. The others did not even take the trouble to
dismount, but stood around waiting. Our men
within were warned by the knocking, for no honest
man up our way ever knocks at a door without coming in, and my father told them all to run for their
lives out the back way, and my mother went to the
door to try to parley and save time for them all to get
away. But my father he said he would not run
like a hunted thing from any rebel, and he stood his
ground.

"Is Dr. Starr at home?" said Whichehalse, and my
mother said, "No." Then he called her a damned
Union woman and told her that she lied; and as she
barred the door-way, he took her by the shoulders
and thrust her aside, and she stumbled on the flat
door-stone and fell upon the grass. And then my
father, seeing this thing, came out himself, flinging
the front door wide open, and asked Whichehalse
what he wanted.

"I want a parcel of Union hounds," said he; "are
you one of them?" But there was no need to ask
this question; for there before them all, lying on the
table in the hall, was the old American flag my
grandfather had brought from Yorktown. And by

this time a few other men, who had not been willing
to leave my father, came out and stood beside him in
the door-way, all unarmed, and my mother put her
arms around my father's neck.

"Fire!" said Whichehalse, only he said more
than this, adding an insult, and then came that
irregular crash of muskets; and so my father, and
three other men, and my dear mother too, were
killed. I have heard that Whichehalse himself fired
the shot that killed her. That was the first volley
that I had heard as I sat with Bill Shelby on the hay.

Then the rebels scattered around the house, and
saw the other men flying, in twos and threes, like
rabbits, toward the mountains. But the rebels on
their horses could make short work of these; and
they galloped across the smooth meadow, picking
our men off one by one, as if it were a deer hunt,
until all but two or three were lying, as I found them,
in little pools of blood among the tussocks. One
man — he was afterwards shot, fighting with the
Union men about Atlanta — escaped by lying in the
water-way below the wheel, in the water among the
long grasses ; and the rushes and the yellow lilies
bent over him, curtain-like, and hid the man from
view. Some six or eight others kept together under
my Uncle Albert, and made a running fight of it, ·
firing back at the rebels on horseback. Each one
of these killed his man, and the two or three that
were not badly shot got safe into the rhododendron
thickets and escaped.

Then Whichehalse called his men back, laughing, from the chase ; and they set fire to the old house, and the mill, and the barn, and all the offices but the distant cow-houses, in one of which, as you know, Bill Shelby had placed me ; and the old flag was burned up where it lay, on the table by the fireside. And after all was done, Whichehalse and his troop rode over the mountains into North Carolina exulting.

I did not dare to come out of the hay-mow until evening, fearing to lose my half dollar, and, besides this, fearing something else, I knew not what, but troubled with the noise. And when it grew dark there was a strange light through the chinks in the barn ; and as I lay there trembling, my Uncle Albert and he that was in the brook came to the door, and called my name softly. They had come back for me. I showed them the half dollar, and they told me to keep it, and that it might help me on my way North.

When we came to the house only one brick wall was standing, and the smoked foundation-stones of the barn ; and we found my father and my dear mother lying, both shot in many places, beside their own front door, with the bodies of the men. None of the neighbors dared to come about ; so we three buried them all, the two men and I, a boy; and I was crying silently, for they did not dare to let me cry aloud. And we started for the North that night with the others, and got safely into the Union lines, where all the men that were left enlisted, and I was sent to Ohio to be put to school.

After the war I heard that Major Whichehalse went back to South Carolina and became a black Republican, and held high office, and came near to being Governor of the State. I have never seen him, and I hope that I never may. Bill Shelby kept me from seeing him that day.

I have often wanted to go back to Laurel Cove, but there are so few people left there that I used to know, and there is a new house and all the rest, I suppose—perhaps even the mill-wheel is gone. But if the old flag were there and had not been burned, my uncle's children could keep it now.

I have never met Bill Shelby, as he called himself, from that day to this. I wonder how they treated him in the band when he went back to them after that day's work ; I fear he may have got into trouble for deserting it. I suppose he was as bad as the rest — perhaps. He was not prominent after the war, like Major Whichehalse. I wish I knew his real name ; I should like to meet him. I owe him one silver half dollar. It was all he had.

June.

Two Passions and a Cardinal Virtue.

A COMEDY OF TWO LONDON JUNES.

DRAMATIS PERSONÆ.

TOM BRUTON.
ARTHUR GORDON.
DUFFUS, afterward LORD PLUMTRE.
MAJOR BRANDYBALL.

MR. WELTERS.
LADY STRANGEWAYS.
LADY MARY MABERLY, afterward
LADY MARY WELTERS.

Walking Gentlemen, and others; Walking Ladies.

ACT I.—JUNE, 1861.

SCENE I.—*A chamber in the Inner Temple.*

(The room is carelessly kept, and full of everything, like that in Dürer's " Melan-colia." There are several book-cases ; leaning up in the corners, or more generally disposed behind pieces of furniture with some effort at conceal-ment, are cricket-bats, tennis-rackets, guns, rods, Indian clubs, polo-mallets, and other sporting articles. In the centre is a table, covered with books bound in law-calf, papers, newspapers, a barrister's wig, and one prominent docu-ment, with " Twistleton v. Gragg, Brief," legibly written on the back. Most of the chairs are also filled with papers and reports. Two large arm-chairs, well worn and precisely alike, are the only unoccupied articles of furniture ; these are placed on either side of the centre-table. R. and L. are two closet doors ; C., the entrance-door of the room.)

(Enter TOM and ARTHUR. They come in without a word, both yawning, and throw back their overcoats, revealing evening dress. Tom crosses to closet R., and Arthur to closet L. ; each throws open a closet door ; the closets are filled with clothing, hanging on hooks, and boots, boxes, and bottles on the floor.)

Tom comes out with a demijohn, and Arthur with a siphon of soda. As they return to the centre-table, Tom sweeps across the top of it with his arm extended straight, brushing off all the books, papers, wig, etc., which fall in a heap on the floor. Arthur picks up the wig and shies it into one of the arm-chairs, then fetches two glasses and places them on the empty table. Tom pours out an inch of brandy in each glass, swinging the demijohn on the back of his arm, and pouring from his shoulder. As he pours, Arthur presses the valve and fills each glass with soda. They simultaneously raise their glasses to their lips. Arthur only sips his, but Tom drinks his glass off and refills it. Both remove their overcoats and take off their boots, which they fling into the vestibule of the entrance-door; each pulls a pair of slippers from under the arm-chair nearest him, puts them on his feet, and throws himself back into the chair. Both sigh. A silence.)

TOM. Well, old man?
    Arthur. Well, old boy?

(Another silence. Tom drinks more brandy-and-soda. As he gets up, he finds that he has been sitting on the wig, which has powdered his trousers. He hurls it savagely into the closet from which he took the demijohn. Arthur lights a cigarette.)

Arthur. Pretty slow to-night, wasn't it?

Tom (grunts affirmation. Then, after a moment, monosyllabically). Sweet champagne.

Arthur. They ought to ice it. *(After a pause, bitterly)* It was the only thing that needed icing.

Tom (looks up quickly at Arthur, who avoids his glance. Who were you talking to, most of the time?

Arthur (carelessly). Oh, I don't know — Miss Moidore, Miss Golding, old Lady Bowler, Giroflé and Giroflà.

Tom (meditatively). They say they give a chromo away with those girls. Who else?

Arthur. No one in particular. Who did you?

Tom (taken by surprise). Why, I—I—oh, I saw Lady Mary, and——

Arthur. So did I.

(Another pause. Tom takes more soda, and Arthur another cigarette. The dawn comes through a window, front, and the light falls on Arthur's face.)

Tom. Arthur, old man, you look pale. You're doing too much of this sort of thing. You're grinding too hard. You can't stand it, the way I can.

Arthur. It's not the work, old boy. *(Takes up the brief.)* Look at that brief — yellow already. It's the last one.

Tom. You keep it on show too long. It gets shopworn. Hasn't old Scrivener sent you anything lately?

Arthur. No. I didn't speak to his daughter at the Manners's.

Tom. That party you danced with Lady Mary?

Arthur. Yes.

Tom. Slow work getting on in our profession.

Arthur (nods).

Tom. Lucky we neither of us want to get married.

Arthur. Yes, yes. *(Rises and walks to the window.)*

Tom (soliloquizing). Now, the Church fellows — they all get good fat livings ; and yet they talk about making them celibate again. I wish Pusey and those chaps would just try the law for a while. We don't get any living. *(Stops and looks at Arthur, who is drumming on the window-pane.)* Now, if a barrister falls in love, he's got to wait till he's sixty before he dare propose. And then the girl don't want him. *(Rises and walks to the closet for another siphon of soda.)* And if she does, it's a chance if he wants her. *(Drinks soda.)* It's too long a term. It's funding

matrimony — that's what it is. And there's not even
a sinking fund — except our hearts. Heigho ! *(Sits
down and takes a pipe.)* Now, most girls want their
bonds — promises to marry — redeemable at sight,
convertible into cash ; offers only considered C. O. D.
They're mercenary creatures. Now, even Lady Mary
—— she's a nice girl.

*Arthur (who all this time has been drumming on the
window-pane, now returns to his seat).* She *is* a nice
girl, Tom.

Tom (puffing at his pipe). I know it. I said so.

Arthur. Tom, do you remember the time when I
dropped the lexicon on Tiffin major's tarts, and you
punched Tiffin major's head because he thrashed me ?

Tom. I do.

Arthur. And the time you got those ribs broken,
playing all Surrey ?

Tom. I rather think I do.

Arthur. And the time we got afloat in the coble
and were picked up by that dirty fisherman ?

Tom. I should think so.

Arthur (draws a long sigh). How the beggar did
starve us, though ! And we half drowned ! Ah,
those were glorious times !

Tom. They were, indeed. But, Arthur, you forget the summer I stayed at your house — after my
father died.

Arthur (quickly). Let's see. How long was that
tart-scrape ago ? Fifteen years ?

Tom. Sixteen.

Arthur. Sixteen years! By Jove! Sixteen years! (*Walks to the window again.*) Tom, old boy, I'm going to quit the law.

Tom (gruffly). Nonsense, young 'un! Wait till that great case—what was it? Twistleton and Gragg —gets into the reports.

Arthur (quietly). Yes, Tom, I'm going to—to Australia.

Tom (starts). The devil! What—what's up? Come, come, youngster, don't get off any more jokes as bad as that one. It's too early in the morning. Wait till court's in session.

Arthur (closes the shutters, which shuts out the dawn and makes the room lighted only by gas light again). Yes, Tom, old boy,—you're the only fellow that I want to tell this to; and perhaps I shouldn't tell you, by daytime,—yes, I am going off—to Van Diemen's Land, to—to have a try at sheep-farming. You ask what's up. It's—it's all up with me, old fellow. (*Sees his glass standing, still full, and drinks it off quickly.*)

Tom (constrainedly). Good Lord, young 'un! has —has Miss Scrivener proposed? (*Laughs.*)

Arthur. I never thought we'd have to cut loose from one another, Tom: it's been very pleasant, knowing you, these sixteen years, old boy. We've had many a long talk late at night, Tom, you and I, and this is the latest of all, perhaps, and the last. I know we shall never talk like this in the daytime, Tom; and (*carelessly*), Tom—you know, I am in love.

Tom (after a pause, slowly). Lady Mary Maberly.

Arthur. Lady Mary Maberly.

Tom (gravely). Arthur, so am I.

Arthur. I knew it, old boy! I knew it! Wish you joy, old boy! you know I do —every joy in the world! *(Rises, and, going to the closet, rattles in it; upsets a box of cigars, picks one of them up, and puts the wrong end in his mouth).*

Tom. Go slow, old man; go slow. How do you know you're not the happy man? *(with a smile).* You can't expect her to ask you, like Miss Scrivener.

Arthur (surprised). Why, Tom, you were with her all the last part of the evening,—I saw you,—and I supposed, of course—— She treated me like an iceberg. I stayed with her as long as I could —nearly all the evening.

Tom (waggishly). Nearly all the evening? And, pray, where were Miss Moidore, and Miss Golding, and old Lady Bowler, and Giroflé and Giroflà? You seemed to talk more of them just now. But, seriously, Arthur, I went up when you left, and very prettily did she snub me in consequence, I can tell you.

Arthur. Ah, Tom, that's all very well; it's very good of you to say these things ; but New Zealand is the place for me: I've quite decided on that.

Tom. A moment ago it was Australia, and just now Van Diemen's Land! *(Seriously)* Arthur, dear boy, if I had your chance of winning Lady Mary Maberly, I—I should be—— *(Tom in turn rises and walks to the window, drumming on the window-pane. A long silence.)*

Arthur. Tom, dear old boy, suppose she loves neither of us?

Tom (laughing). That, old man, is quite impossible.

Arthur. Tom, you'll excuse gush, but I'm not sure I don't care a good deal for you, just the same. Suppose ——

Tom. Thanks, old chap. Same to you *(Salutes).*

Arthur. Suppose — we're neither of us very rich ——

Tom (decisively). Lady Mary don't care for money.

Arthur (angrily). Of course not! Don't be a fool. I was going to say, we mustn't have any row, you know,— any dispute,— any angry words, even.

Tom. We won't have any row.

Arthur. We must back each other up all we can, and then let the best man win.

Tom. And the one that don't win will be " best man," hey? Here's to the wedding! Your hand on it, old fellow!

Arthur. Your hand on it! though you're the one, Tom, I know very well.

Tom. Not by a jugful, old man. I only wish you could have seen her snub me! and then the way she looked after you, when you went off with Miss Moidore!

Arthur. Did she? did she really look after me?

Tom. Aha! Price of wool gone down in Van Diemen's Land, eh?

Arthur (savagely). Don't make an ass of yourself, Tom. I'll only wait over a steamer or so, to make sure you're the man and wish you joy. Tom, I've got ten thousand pounds, more or less.   How much have you?

Tom. Eight.

Arthur. Tom Bruton, I've got a proposition.   We put the eighteen thousand in a common pot; the man who wins her keeps all but one thousand, which you give to me to start me off with.   We can't have Lady Mary marry too poor a fellow, though she doesn't care for money.   She must be treated like a lady. Heigho! we're none too rich between us.

Tom. But you've got ten thousand, and I've got only eight.

Arthur (hastily). Never mind about details.   How shall we tell—how shall we determine whom she loves?   That is the main question, after all.

Tom. I don't know.   *(As if an idea struck him)* Heads or tails?

Arthur. Nonsense, Tom!   Don't jest about it.

Tom. It can't be hard to find out.   There must be some way, if she cares for either of us *(reflectively).* We might even ask her, you know.

Arthur. Let the next party decide it.   Where do we see her next?

Tom. Shropshire House.

Arthur. Shropshire House —even if we have to ask her.   This suspense must be ended.   It is terrible to be enemies.   Tom, you must ask her first.

Tom. No, no, Arthur: you take first try.   *(He goes to the window and opens it; the broad sunlight streams in.)*   Poor boy, you look pale!

Arthur. So much the more chance for you, old fellow!

Tom. Go to bed, Arthur ; go to bed. I'll see old Scrivener if he comes.

Arthur. No, no, Tom ; too much trouble. I'll take it out in wet towels this time; I've been a lazy fellow, you know, these sixteen years. Tom, my boy *(he puts one hand on each of Tom's shoulders, and looks at him a moment)*, I'm sorry it's coming so soon.

SCENE II.— *A Club in Pall-Mall.*

(MAJOR BRANDYBALL, sitting in the window, with a bottle of soda-water. Men keep coming in and passing through the room ; they all nod to the major. Tables covered with newspapers, glasses, etc. In the foreground an old gentleman, sitting on a pile of newspapers, asleep.)

(Enter First Gentleman, L.)

How are you, major ?

Major. How are you ?

(First Gentleman comes forward and picks up the newspapers from the table, one after the other. Not finding the one he wants, he tries to pull one out from under the gentleman in the chair. A loud snore is the only response. Enter Second Gentleman.)

Second Gentleman. How d'ye do, major ?

Major. How d'ye do ?

(Second Gentleman goes up to written placard on the wall. Enter Third Gentleman.)

Third Gent. Halloo, major !

Major. Halloo, Charlie !

(Charlie comes forward and passes First Gentleman ; each stares at the other.)

First Gent. What's new, major ?

Major. Nothing much.

First Gent. Lord Strangeways got his divorce, I hear.

Major. It's all in the evening paper.

First Gent. Yes, and old Snawker's *on* the evening paper. I'd like to light 'em up under the old hulk, some day. *(False exit.)*

Third Gent. Who's that fellow who just went out?

Major. He's a member here : that's young——

Second Gent. (interrupting). I see that fellow Welters is up here.

First Gent. (returning at the remark). Yes, I saw it too — with some surprise, I confess.

Third Gent. (joining the group in the window). Who's Welters? *(Stares again at First Gentleman.)*

Major (dryly). Ah, Charlie—Mr. *(mumbles)*, Mr. *(mumbles ; pantomime of introduction of Third Gentleman to First Gentleman. Both look at each other angrily).* Oh, Welters is a fellow in the City; made no end of money.

Second Gent. Contractor?

First Gent. Cotton-broker?

Major. No : stock-broker, I believe.

Both. Oh !

Major. Friends of the Lauristons.

All. Ah !

Second Gent. Pretty girl, that Lady Mary Maberly.

First Gent. Bad year, this, for pretty girls.

(Duffus enters L.; nods to the group in the window ; Third Gentleman leaves and joins him. They walk forward. The others draw together more closely and speak a little lower.)

Second Gent. Now, whom do you suppose, major, they can enter that girl for? Nothing under a cup will set old Lauriston on his legs.

Major. I saw young Arthur Gordon with her a good deal, last night.

First Gent. Tom Bruton's pretty sweet that way, I fancy.

Second Gent. Now, I wonder if those fellows are asses enough to think they can get that girl? Take my word for it, Welters is the man. I see Strangeways is backing him here. Strangeways, you know, is the old lady's brother. Welters put him into stocks.

Major. Nice girl is Lady Mary — nice girl as ever was. I don't know much about Welters.

Duffus to Third Gent. (walking forward). What do you know about her family?

Third Gent. Very respectable; one of the best in the island. No end of go in her, too. Lady Lauriston was a St. Leger.

Duffus. So poor old Strangeways has got out of his scrape at last.

Third Gent. So I see. Pretty nearly ruined, too. Well, well! that comes of marrying a girl without a penny. She always gets even with you by spending yours.

Duffus. Perhaps you don't look quite so close, either, if she has all the pennies; eh, eh?

Third Gent. Ha, ha! Let's read the trial. *(Pulls newspaper from under Snawker; in doing so, shakes the handkerchief off his head. Snawker opens his eyes and looks around confusedly.)*

First Gent. (in the window). Look at Strangeways' new ponies. Well, well! I bet on Welters, every time.
(All rush to the window and look out, except the major.)

Major. For a pony?
Second Gent. For a pony if you like.
Major. Done. *(They take out their books and note it. Enter Tom and Arthur, L.)* Egad, for once in my life I'll back young lovers against old money-bags: ha, ha!
All. Halloo, Gordon! How are you, Bruton?
Tom and Arthur. How are you, major! How are you? *(Exeunt.)*
Third Gent. (front, reading the newspaper). Here's the place; here's her evidence; Strangeways' counsel cross-examines.
(All look over his shoulder eagerly.)

SCENE III.—*Shropshire House.*

(A conservatory, brilliantly lighted. C., a wide door, open, through which dancing is occasionally seen in a distant room. R. and L., two large banana palms. Front, a low ottoman, shaded by a mass of orange-trees. Throughout the scene there is a nearly continuous sound of music from the dancing-room. Ladies and gentlemen keep passing through, arm in arm; now and then a footman with a tray of negus or ices. Enter LADY LAURISTON with LADY MARY MABERLY.)

Lady Mary. See, mamma! isn't the conservatory lovely?

Lady Lauriston. Yes, dear ; almost like the one in Pinelands.

Lady Mary. And, oh ! just look at those banana-trees ! Aren't they superb?

Lady Lauriston. Ah, my dear, we had much finer ones before your papa had to sell Pinelands.

(Lady Mary keeps looking about among the shrubs, as if expecting some one, but pretending to be examining the plants and flowers. Arthur appears from behind one of the palms and approaches Lady Lauriston. Lady Mary takes a step forward; just then Brandyball passes through from R. to C.; and Lady Lauriston, who has pretended not to see Arthur, advances to meet Brandyball.)

Lady Lauriston. Ah, dear major ! a familiar face at last. *(Arthur stands front and bites his lips.)* Mary, my dear, you know Major Brandyball, I am sure ; one of my oldest friends.

(The major bows and smiles. Lady Mary murmurs, " Delighted, I am sure," and looks at Arthur; the major also looks at Arthur, and makes as if he would escape.)

Lady Lauriston. Come, major, we can't let you off in this way. You must give my daughter your arm. One is really in need of protection in this house ; there is positively no one here we know. *(Looks at Arthur.)*

Major (bowing again, and repeating Lady Mary's words). Delighted, I am sure.

(Exeunt, leaving Arthur standing alone in the room. As soon as they disappear, Arthur flings himself upon the ottoman and covers his face in his hands. A burst of music is heard from the dancing-room.)

Tom (coming out from behind the other palm-tree). Never mind, old fellow. Cheer up. Never mind the Dowager *(placing his hand on Arthur's shoulder, who is still inconsolable).* You're not going to marry the Dowager.

Arthur. Ah, old boy, I told you so. It's no use. She might have spoken to me instead of old Brandy-ball.

Tom. Nonsense! How could she, when her mother shot her at him in that fashion? Unless I'm much mistaken, old Brandyball didn't like the job.

Arthur (savagely). She'd flirt with anybody.

Tom. Come, old man, none of that! You forget she's my girl too. Look out! here they come.

(Both dodge back hastily, each behind a palm-tree. Enter the MAJOR *and* LADY MARY, L.*)*

Major. So you don't like society, eh!

Lady Mary (ingenuously). I think I'm just beginning to learn to like it.

Major. Ah, it's a great thing,— I may say, the only thing,—when you get used to it. I fancy you're not much out yet?

Lady Mary. Oh, but indeed we go to two or three houses every night.

Major. And don't the men treat you well? Ah, Lady Mary, you can't make me believe that.

Lady Mary. I don't much care for the men — especially the younger men. They're so stupid, and they have so little to say for themselves.

Major. Ah, poor things! they say a great deal too much for themselves, sometimes. Well, my young lady, you'll come to it in time — when you've bagged a few of these same young men : *l'appétit vient en mangeant ;* it's not bad sport.

(An elderly gentleman, and a young lady elegantly dressed, pass across the stage from R. to L. The major rises and bows.)

Lady Mary. Who was that ?

Major. Don't you know the Duke of Trapping-ton? That was his new duchess. Her mother was a cook.

Lady Mary. How can such creatures come into society ?

Major. Beauty, dear Lady Mary ; 'tis their beauty does it. Duke looks well to-night ; doesn't show his years.

Lady Mary. I thought the duchess was rather — rather ——

Major. Yes, I understand — a little vulgar, per-haps, or, rather, over-dressed. But, dear me, what can you expect when you think of her origin ? Beau-tiful arms, though — for pasties. Eh, eh ?

Lady Mary (is silent a moment). How quiet it is here !

Major. Yes, yes ; a little lonely, perhaps. Shall we — shall we go into the dancing-room ?

(They rise, and cross R.)

Arthur (sotto voce, to Tom, behind the palm-trees). Go in, Tom.

(Tom follows after them. Enter LADY LAURISTON. She meets Arthur, who does not expect her to recognize him.)

Lady Lauriston. Ah, Mr. —— How do you do,

Mr. Gordon? I was afraid —— Ah, you have not seen Lady Mary?

Arthur (with studied politeness). I have not had the pleasure of meeting Lady Mary. I saw her a moment ago——

Lady Lauriston. With Major Brandyball?

Arthur. With Tom Bruton.

Lady Lauriston (agitated). Which way did they go?

Arthur. That way, I believe (*showing Lady Lauriston L., the opposite direction to the one Tom had taken*).

(*Exit Lady Lauriston. Enter* TOM *and* LADY MARY, R. *Lady Mary is blushing violently. She is holding a red rose in one hand, and looking straight before her.*)

Arthur. Ah! (*sighs deeply, and exit, C., toward the dancing.*)
(*Tom and Lady Mary sit down.*)

Tom. And so, Lady Mary, we decided — Arthur and I — that we should see you to-night, and ask——
(*Enter* LADY LAURISTON, L., *hastily.*)

Lady Lauriston. Oh, my dear, where have you been all this time? The Earl of Goodwood has been asking for you, and young Dick Porto, and Mr. Bullion says you positively promised him the last dance.

Lady Mary. Mamma, surely you remember Mr. Bruton.

Lady Lauriston. Pray forgive me, Mr. Bruton. I — would you kindly mind getting me some seltzer?

It is really very warm. *(Exit Tom.)* Mary, I am positively ashamed of you. The Duke of Trapping-ton——

Lady Mary. I hate the Duke of Trappington !

Lady Lauriston. Why, when did you ever see him? His Grace was kind enough to ask if I had a daughter in society. Here comes Miss Maggot.

(Enter a thin, swarthy young lady, much décolletée, with DUFFUS *in full uniform.)*

Ah, my dear Miss Maggot — so charmed at last——

(Miss Maggot is quite taken up with her cavalier, and passes by without heeding Lady Lauriston.)

How such a person can ever have worked her way into society — but, my dear Mary, money will do everything nowadays. I hear she is one of the most fashionable girls in town. Come, we must go back ; I haven't seen you dance this evening. I think the duke —— *(Exeunt.)*

(Enter TOM, *with a glass of water,* L. ; ARTHUR, R.)

Both (together). Did you give her that rose?

Tom. Where are they?

Arthur. Gone with young Duffus, I fancy.

Tom (throws his glass of seltzer into the orange-trees, angrily). Her mother only wanted to get rid of me. I didn't give her the rose. I'd only just begun ; had hardly started ——

Arthur. It *was* Duffus, then.

(Both exeunt, in different directions. Enter the MAJOR *and* LADY MARY.)

Major. You seem to like this conservatory.

Lady Mary. It is so pleasant and cool after the ball-room.

Major. Devilish pleasant — and deuced cool. I suspect young Duffus didn't find it so when he came in here a few minutes ago. If ever man was potted, he was. She's a lucky girl.

Lady Mary. Whom do you mean?

Major. That Maggot woman. I believe she's going to marry young Duffus.

Lady Mary. Do you mean that young man in uniform who just passed through? Impossible! He's a mere boy.

Major. My dear young lady, think of the title. Who could resist it? He will be Earl of Plumtre one of these days. It's a fashionable title, too. Rank will do anything.

Lady Mary (sighs). I'm afraid you're all very worldly, major. First you said it was beauty; then mamma said it was money; and now it is rank.

Major. Never mind, my dear girl; you'll learn it in time. I remember when your moth—other ladies who were just like you once. And they all say you're to be the fashion this year.

(*Enter* Tom, L., *and goes behind a palm-tree.*)

And I'm sure, if you'll suffer a compliment from an old man like me ——

(*Enter* Arthur, R., *diffidently.*)

Arthur. Good-evening, Lady Mary. I ——
Lady Mary. Good-evening, Mr. Gordon.

Arthur. I'm so glad to meet you this evening. I — I —— How do you do, major?

Major (gravely). How do you do, Gordon? *(Throughout the conversation he watches Gordon closely.)*

Arthur. I wanted to tell you that — eh ——

(Lady Mary looks down, twirling the rosebud. Arthur stammers and recovers himself.)

It is a very pleasant party, is it not, Lady Mary?

Lady Mary. Delightful.

Major. So pleasant to see you young people enjoy yourselves! You were about to say ——

Arthur. Oh, yes: I — I wanted to tell you that I met Lady Lauriston, and she told me to — that is, I was about to ask you to — to dance, Lady Mary.

Lady Mary. Thank you, but it is very hot. I am resting.

Major. I must go back to Lady Lauriston. *(Exit.)*

Arthur. I wished very much to tell you ——

Major (going out the wide door, C., meets Lady Lauriston). Have you seen your daughter, Lady Lauriston?

Lady Lauriston. No; is she not in there?

Major. No; I think she is in the ball-room. May I take you there?

(Their voices cease to be heard in the distance.)

Arthur. That — that I loved you, Mary ——

Lady Mary. Ah! *(She rises hastily; a long pause; both are standing.)*

Arthur. Will you not tell me?

Major (heard speaking loudly in the distance). I surely thought they were in the dancing-room ; they must have.left just as we entered.

Lady Mary. Oh, I hear my mother ! I must go !

Arthur. Will you not tell me?   *(He seizes her hand.)*

Lady Mary. Oh, I do not know !   Oh, let me go !

(She breaks away from Arthur, and goes in the direction of the major's voice.)

Major (entering the door, C.). Is Lady Mary here ?

Lady Mary (to Arthur, softly, as if answering the major). Yes.

(As she goes to meet the major, she drops her rose upon the floor, near Arthur. Exit Lady Mary, with the major. Arthur seizes the rose and kisses it, then holds it in his hands, looking at it rapturously. Tom comes out from behind the palm-tree. Arthur drops his hand, looking at him.)

Tom. Congratulate you, dear Arthur.

Arthur. Tom !

Tom. Good — good-bye, old fellow. *(Goes to the door, C.; figures are seen passing, to waltz-music.)*

Arthur. Where are you going? *(Starts after him ; Tom waves him back.)* What are you going to do ?

Tom. I'm going — sheep-farming,— in Van Diemen's Land. *(Exit hastily.)*

Act II.—June, 1881.

SCENE I.— *Boudoir in the house of Lady Mary Welters.* LADY MARY WELTERS ; LADY STRANGEWAYS.

Lady Mary (laying down the paper listlessly). Who is this man they call the Nugget?

Lady Strangeways (eagerly). Why, what of him? Has he been doing anything new?

Lady Mary. New? No. Always the same. I can't take up a paper but I read about the Nugget. I am weary of him. I haven't a friend who calls that doesn't tell me about the Nugget.

Lady Strangeways. Except Plumtre?

Lady Mary (impatiently). Except Plumtre, of course. All my male friends are friends of the Nugget ; all the women rave about him ; even Plumtre is to dine with him to-night. Last week he outbid me at a charity ball ; this week he wins poor Welters's last guinea at the Club ; in short, he has done everything to me but leave his card.

Lady Strangeways. That is odd ; because he told me the other day that he particularly wanted to meet you.

Lady Mary. He is unusually slow, then, in effecting this particular wish. Not that I care to see him. Who is he? — some ordinary *nouveau-riche?*

Lady Strangeways. Rather extraordinary, I fancy. Sir Thomas Edgecomb is not a chance favorite of

Fortune, if I am any judge.   In the first place, he is
a gentleman ; in the second place, he is unusually
handsome ; and in the third place, I am a little afraid
of him.

Lady Mary. Ha, ha ! ha, ha, ha !   Gilda, that is
the best yet.   The Nugget rich and handsome, and
you afraid of him !   He must be the devil !

Lady Strangeways (lighting a cigarette). No *(puffing)*, not the devil, I fancy.   You and I should know
him when we see him.   Ah! here comes Plumtre.
Good-morning, Plum.

(Enter EARL PLUMTRE. *Crosses* L. *to Lady Strangeways, and bows ; then* R.
to Lady Mary, and kisses her hand.)

Lady Strangeways. Well   done,   Plum !   Didn't
know you had so much *aplomb*.   But look out : it's
too *soigneux*, too *grand seigneur* — won't do to-
day — bad form, I am afraid — too theatrical, you
know.

Plumtre. And doesn't Lord Strangeways do the
same by you, Lady Strangeways ?   I had thought a
gentleman of the old school ——

Lady Strangeways. Old school, indeed !   I have
always felt Strangeways an anachronism in this reign.
Now, under King Billy, a bootjack or two wouldn't
have signified.   Kiss my hand, indeed !

Plumtre. Pray let me repair his omission.

Lady Strangeways. Nay, I am Lady Mary's friend,
you know, and was a poor country-girl before I was
married, and an innocent one.

Lady Mary. Before you were married. — Pray,
Plumtre, who is the Nugget ?

Plumtre. Sir Thomas Edgecomb; one of the oldest baronetcies in Ireland; wealth unknown; good hand at whist, poker, and baccarat; clubs, Carlton and Travellers'; knows everybody——

Lady Mary. Except me——

Plumtre. And the queen. But he is to be presented at court next week, and desires your acquaintance to-night.

Lady Mary. Which he shall not have. (*Rising*) Good-bye, Lord Plumtre; I am tired. Lady Strangeways will entertain you. Look after him, Gilda. (*Gathers up her work, and exit.*)

Plumtre. Well, I'm damned! What's put her out to-day, Lady Strangeways? What's Edgecomb done, that she's so down on him?

Lady Strangeways. Perhaps it's his coming to see her.

Plumtre. Impossible! Edgecomb's a man to know.

Lady Strangeways. Perhaps, then, it's his not coming to see her.

Plumtre (with a start). You think so? (*Recovering himself*) No, that's impossible, too. (*Strokes his mustache.*)

Lady Strangeways. You think so? A word of advice, Lord Plumtre.

Plumtre. What?

Lady Strangeways. Lean forward — forward — forward still! (*Plumtre is a little awkward; she whispers close in his ear, but in a loud voice.*) Keep your eye on Lady Mary, Plumtre. (*Exit, laughing.*)

Plumtre. Now, what the deuce does she mean by that? *(Reflectively)* Pretty girl, Gilda Strangeways. I remember, down in Devonshire, when she was Gilda Trevethick —— Halloo, here's Welters!

(Enter WELTERS, *in an overcoat, his eyes red, face sunken and slightly flushed.)*

Welters. Halloo, Plumtre! you here?

Plumtre (dryly). Yes.

Welters. Seen her ladyship?

Plumtre. Lady Mary is indisposed this morning.

Welters. Egad, so am I. That Nugget is the devil. Fancy, he has just been backing Trappington at whist. But I thought I heard some one talking as I came in?

Plumtre. Lady Strangeways has just left the room.

Welters. Coddling up Lady Mary, I'll be bound. Plumtre, that woman has a bad influence on my wife. As if it were a fellow's fault that the luck has been against him! I had money enough when she married me. That woman is extravagant enough to break a Rothschild.

Plumtre. Lady Mary, or Lady Strangeways?

Welters. Lady Mary, of course. Lady Strangeways may go to the devil for me. I guess old Strangeways knows the way as well as I do. Ha, ha! eh? Have some brandy — a pick-me-up. *(Rings.)*

Plumtre. Thank you, not for me.

(A footman enters, bearing a tray.)

Welters. You'd better. *(Fills two glasses.)* Plumtre, what are you to do with a woman like that?

Plumtre (sipping his glass). Like what?

Welters. Like my wife. Curse it, that comes of marrying a poor girl. I don't see why I did it.

Plumtre. Because you wanted to get into society.

Welters (stares stupidly). Curse it, Plumtre, that's insulting.

Plumtre. You think so? *(Scans Welters coolly.)*

Welters. But damn it, Plumtre, what am I to do? It's been a bad year for me. That Nugget fellow has won two thousand more.

Plumtre. Make some money.

Welters. There again! he suggested my buying into an Australian cattle company, and the shares haven't been quoted for three weeks. Well, I must be going. Coming round to the Club?

Plumtre. By and by.

Welters. Ta ta. *(Starts to go; turns at the door and comes back.)* I say, Plumtre, you couldn't make · it convenient to let me have a hundred or so—till to-morrow?

Plumtre. Certainly. How much shall it be?

Welters. Well, make it two. I'll pay you Saturday. Thanks. Good-morning. *(Takes more brandy, and exit.)*

Plumtre. Poor Lady Mary! Ah, here she is!

(Reënter LADY MARY.*)*

Your husband has just gone.

Lady Mary. Ah!

Plumtre. He has been playing again — with Edge-comb.

Lady Mary. Again that man! And he lost, of course?

Plumtre. I suppose so. *(Watching her)* He borrowed some money of me.

Lady Mary (colors violently). Of you! And he is my husband! *(Aside.)*

Plumtre. Alas!

Lady Mary (abruptly). Good-bye. I am going for a drive.

Plumtre. Will you not ride with me?

Lady Mary. No, I cannot. I must make some visits.

Plumtre. When shall I see you again?

Lady Mary. I do not know. *(At the door)* I shall drive in the Park at six. *(Exit.)*

Plumtre (alone, looking after her). And there goes the most fashionable woman in London! Well, well! She plays the part well enough; lots of go in her; plenty of spirit, too. 'Gad, her look when she found her lord and master had borrowed money of me was divine — simply divine. All the same, I'm glad I never married. There's Gilda Strangeways, now — poor old Strangeways' second shot. He got divorced from his first one, — let me see, it must be nearly twenty years ago, — and then he tried it again with a younger one. What's that the Frenchmen say? there are three things a sensible man never need trouble himself with — a yacht, a house in the country, and —— Halloo, major!

(Enter Major Brandyball, after a footman.)

Major. There, there, my good fellow. I know very well Lady Mary isn't in. I can wait. Halloo, Plumtre! you here, as usual?

Plumtre. I just dropped in to ask Lady Mary if— if——

Major. If Welters had got home yet. Just so. Sorry you missed him.

Plumtre. I—I think Lady Mary's gone to drive, major.

Major. I don't suppose she's gone to Boulogne— yet. I can wait. But don't you stay on my account. How's Welters?

Plumtre. Welters is in a bad way, I fear; been losing more money to Edgecomb. That Nugget's the devil.

Major. Ah, it was a bad day for poor Lady Mary when she married Welters. Old Lady Lauriston forced her into it, I fancy; but the girl was willing enough. She kept Pinelands, and gave up her daughter.

Plumtre. A girl's got to marry somebody.

Major. Yes, yes, just so; but she needn't marry Welters. Pity he doesn't die, though, and give some of you fellows a chance. There, there, Plumtre! don't look so frightened; don't go!

Plumtre. I must. Good-bye. *(Exit.)*

Major (alone). There's a fine fellow for you, now, and a crony of the Prince's. Well, well, I'm getting old; and so's her Majesty; and our fashions come from

France and Newmarket. What can Edgecomb want of Mary Welters now, I wonder? Edgecomb's a sensible fellow; and yet he seems as much crazed after this fashionable set as any tailor's son with a brand-new fortune. He surely knew Mary Maberly in old times. Yet he wants me to present him. Thinks she's forgotten him, I suppose. Now, I should think she must remember Tom Bruton. Halloo, here she comes!

(Enter Lady Mary.*)*

Lady Mary. Ah, major, you here? This is jolly! I'm so glad I returned. Calling on women is awfully slow — for a woman.

Major. Lady Mary, I have come as an ambassador to-day from a young — at least a younger — friend of mine. He pines, like all the world, to know you, but, unlike all the world, does not know you. Or rather, he says he doesn't.

Lady Mary. Oh, well, I shall be delighted, of course. Who is he?

Major. He has but lately returned from Australia. His name is Edgecomb.

Lady Mary. The Nugget again! The town seems full of that ubiquitous creature. I am weary of him.

Major. But you don't know him yet?

Lady Mary. I know enough of him. A man who takes all London by storm, and doesn't come near me for three months!

Major. That shows his prudence. He keeps his most dangerous venture for the last.

Lady Mary (wearily). Well, well, bring him to-night. *A propos*, if you know him—do you know him well?

Major. As well as one can know a man of forty who chooses to keep his soul to himself.

Lady Mary. I wish you'd stop Welters from playing with him. Good-bye. I must dress for my drive. Remember, Welters plays too high. *(Exit.)*

Major (looking after her). And I wish she'd stop playing—with Plumtre. Lady Welters plays too high.

SCENE II.— *The Club, as in Act I.*

(Several gentlemen standing at the window. SNAWKER *sitting on a pile of newspapers, as in Act I.* SIR THOMAS EDGECOMB *at a table, smoking. Enter* STRANGEWAYS.)

First Gent. Halloo. Strangeways! how was the meeting?

Strangeways. Haven't you heard? Chartreuse first ; Blueblood second.

Second Gent. And Mademoiselle Fifi?

Strangeways. Distanced.

First Gent. Hm! Bad for Welters.

Strangeways. Welters got it pretty heavy here last night, I'm told.

First Gent. 'Sh! there's the Nugget. *(Points over his shoulder with his thumb at Edgecomb.)*

Second Gent. Have you dined yet? Come in to dinner.

Strangeways. The Prince was there.

(Exeunt, talking. Enter MAJOR BRANDYBALL.*)*

Major. Halloo, Tom!   Have some soda?

(Rings a bell. A footman enters and takes the order. Snawker rises and goes out, yawning.)

Edgecomb. Well, major, what result?

Major. Lady Mary Welters will receive you to-night. *(Both drink; a long pause.)* Tom, I can't understand this desire of yours to meet Lady Mary.

Edgecomb. I used to know her in old times.

Major. I fear her old times were better than her new ones.   But if you knew her, why take such a roundabout way of seeing her again?

Edgecomb (with a hard laugh). I wish to prepare her — for the surprise.

Major (dryly). Lady Mary is never surprised.   She surprises. *(Another long pause. The major looks at him curiously.)*   In old times, you say.   Let me see: in the old times wasn't there another of you?

Edgecomb. Gordon, you mean?

Major. Yes, Gordon — Arthur Gordon.   Let me see: what became of him?

Edgecomb. Dead.

Major. Dead, is he?   I knew he hadn't been in town these ten years.   Dead, you say?   I'm sorry for it.   I used to think he cared a little for Lady Mary — when she was Lady Mary Maberly.

Edgecomb. He used to think so, too.   I am sorry, too — for that.

Major. You're a bitter fellow, Bruton — Sir Thomas, I mean. Now, if you'd stopped in town, instead of going to the bush, you'd have got a little cynical, a little skeptical — that's all. But that doesn't explain to me why you want to see Lady Mary again. Perhaps you loved her too?

Edgecomb. Love isn't the only passion one has for a woman.

Major. True. There is the desire of being fashionable, for instance. But I don't think you care for that. There's the desire of ruining her, besides. That's also rather in fashion.

Edgecomb. Arthur and I both loved her, major. And I loved Arthur. I have given up the habit since. It is a pretty little game enough, for a boy; but sometimes it happens that the stakes are too heavy for one side.

Major. And then he has to give it up. Just so.

Edgecomb. Do you happen to remember how Arthur gave it up?

Major. She refused him, I suppose.

Edgecomb. Not at first, but more than that. It was this way. We both loved her in those days; and we both found it out. But I think I cared as much for Arthur as for her. So we agreed that she should choose between us, which one she loved herself, and the other was to go to Australia. And I went to Australia.

Major. Just so. And Arthur stayed to marry the girl. Why didn't he?

Edgecomb. I thought he had.   I thought he had, for many years ; only it seemed a little strange that he didn't write to me.   It was not like Arthur not to write to me.   Arthur himself was my one pleasant thought all those years.   I wasn't exactly happy, you know,— I gave up that sort of thing with the other when I went to Van Diemen's Land,— but it was always very pleasant to me to think of Arthur's happiness, and that the girl we both loved was happy with him.   So I thought of this all the time for some eight years or so ; I had not much else to think of, alone in Australia.

Major. I thought it was Van Diemen's Land?

Edgecomb. Our first notion had been Van Diemen's Land ; but when I first got there Arthur sent me all the money he could spare, and I started a sheep-farm in Australia.   I knew that Arthur could never have forgotten me ; and, after all, it was natural enough he did not write, after the first. He must have known well enough that his happiness could never be a pain to me ; but he was a delicate, sensitive fellow, not a rough customer like me, and had the tact to try and help me to forget.   I had a hard, rough life those eight years ; I never went to the cities, much less met any one from England.   It was a hard struggle, and I had my times of discouragement.   At such times I used to comfort myself with thinking of Arthur.   One of us was happy, at least ; and I felt it was proper enough that he should be the one.   I was better made for fighting, you see.   Well, on one such night of discouragement, when I was thinking of him, and of her — it was a cold June evening, I remember ——

Major. Your cigar is out. Have a light?

Edgecomb. Thanks. I was sitting by the fire, and my men brought up word that they had found a man — a tramp, as they supposed — in the bush, asking for me. He had wandered from the trail in the dark, and was pretty well done up. So they brought up a man, almost in rags he appeared, and miserably ill. I never recognized him; but it was Arthur Gordon. She had kept him at reach for several years, playing with him; she may have cared for him or not; I do not know. But in the end she married Welters. Arthur had tried it in London a year or two without her. Then he threw up the sponge and came out to Australia after me. All this he told me in the night, with a broken voice, from time to time, as he found strength to speak. He never could bear to write to me, he said; and just about sunrise he looked up with a trace of his old smile and died in my arms. I stayed in Australia ten years longer; I was just beginning to make my fortune at that time.

Major. Poor Arthur!

Edgecomb. Arthur was dead; but in those ten years I thought the more of Lady Mary. At last the thought became too strong for me, and I came back to England to meet her. I have been watching her for these three months. Now can you fancy why I wish to meet her?

Major. Poor Lady Mary!

Edgecomb (stops to light his cigar again). I may as
well tell you, major; you are a man of the world.
All that was kindly in me was buried, you see —
buried with Arthur in the bush.   But I live; and
whatever strength I have I have saved for this one
purpose — a purpose shaped and forged in these ten
long, lonely years.   Major, I will meet that woman
again, no longer poor and unknown, weak and well-
meaning, as I was.   The devil's help is with me now,
and stays with me until I ruin her.   I'll ruin her
husband, ruin her, and cast her nature, naked and
revealed, before the scorn of that same false world
she worshipped so.   By God, I'll win once more
that miserable love of hers, and cast it back at her
with a jest; I'll play with it awhile, as she with
Arthur, and then — and then—— Here comes
Welters.

(*Enter* WELTERS, STRANGEWAYS, *and the two gentlemen.*)

How are you, Welters? you're not at home to-night?

Welters (surlily). Lady Mary is at home, I believe.
I'm not.   Will you play to-night?

Edgecomb. To-morrow, perhaps; to-night I'm going to your house.   That is *(turning to the major)*, if
the major will go there to present me — now.

Major (looks at Edgecomb.   After a pause). I shall
be charmed, I am sure.

(*Exeunt the major and Edgecomb.   The others sit down at a card-table.*)

SCENE III.—*A drawing-room at Mr. Welters's.* PLUMTRE *and* LADY MARY WELTERS, *seated on a sofa.*

Plumtre. Is it to be to-morrow, then? I'll have the horses ready.

Lady Mary. It may be to-morrow; it may be never. Do not press me so.

Plumtre. I adore you!

Lady Mary (rises, with a movement of impatience, and touches a bell. Enter footman). Is your master at home?

Footman. He told me to say he was at the Club, your ladyship. He will not be in this evening, your ladyship.

Lady Mary. That will do.

(Reseats herself. While she is talking with Plumtre, guests begin to arrive.)

Plumtre. You are charming to-night. The Prince spoke of you to-day.

Lady Mary (languidly). Did he?

(Enter LORD *and* LADY STRANGEWAYS.*)*

Lady Strangeways. How do, Mary?

Lady Mary. How do, aunt?

Lord Strangeways. Delighted to see you looking so well. *(Nods distantly to Plumtre.)* Where's Welters?

Lady Mary. I do not know.

(As they are talking, other guests enter and fall into groups. Finally, MAJOR BRANDYBALL *comes in with* EDGECOMB. *The major approaches Lady Mary; Edgecomb stands at a distance, looking at her.)*

Major. Lady Mary, I have kept my promise. I wish to present to you the friend of whom I spoke this afternoon.

Plumtre (sotto voce). That damned Edgecomb again !

(*All fall aside as Edgecomb steps up.*)

Major. Lady Mary Welters, Sir Thomas Edgecomb.

(*They bow. The others walk back, leaving Lady Mary and Sir Thomas in the centre.*)

Edgecomb. Lady Mary, I have long wished to meet you. I have a message for you — a commission to perform.

Lady Mary. Indeed, Sir Thomas? I—I didn't know we had anything in common.

Edgecomb. We have — or, rather, we had once, Lady Mary.

Lady Mary. You can't imagine how you excite my curiosity. What is it?

Edgecomb. I can hardly tell you now. May I venture to call to-morrow?

Lady Mary. To-morrow I shall hardly be at home. We have that charity-bazaar, you know.

Plumtre (approaching). To-morrow night it is, then ?

Lady Mary (after a moment's hesitation). To-morrow night. (*To Edgecomb*) I shall be at Shropshire House to-morrow, Sir Thomas. Shall I see you there? (*Exit on Edgecomb's arm.*)

Lady Strangeways (to Plumtre). Look out for Mary, Plum. They say the Nugget's a dangerous man.

Plumtre. If you have already found him so, I am safe, Lady Strangeways.

First Gentleman (to stranger). That was our great London beauty—Lady Mary Welters.

Stranger. Indeed? She's prettier than the photographs.

First Gent. They say she's rather fast.

Plumtre (to Lady Strangeways). How did your husband get here, Lady Strangeways? I just left him at a theatre in Miss Coralie's box.

Lady Strangeways. You look after Lady Mary, Plum. I'll take care of Strangeways. She's gone off with the Nugget.

(Exit Plumtre. Re-enter LADY MARY *with* MAJOR BRANDYBALL.)

Lady Mary. I don't owe you thanks for your friend, major. He's just like all the rest.

Major (dryly). Is he?

Lady Mary. While he kept to himself he was interesting ; I began to be a little afraid of him. But when he begins to make love to me he makes a fool of himself, like any other.

Major. Not quite like another, I fancy. Try him again. Here he comes.

Elgecomb (approaching). I hope the major has not been telling evil tales of my youth, Lady Mary. They are idle stories, believe me. You must let me correct them.

(He leads Lady Mary to a chair, and sits down beside her. Reënter PLUMTRE.)

Plumtre (to the major). What sort of a fellow is that Edgecomb, major? Did you bring him here?

Lady Strangeways. Don't answer him, major. Lord Plumtre is a grasping monopolist. Have you seen Strangeways, Plum?

Plumtre. You were to look after him, Lady Strangeways. I think he's got away.

Lady Strangeways. Gone to that Mrs. Mayfly's, I'll be bound. *(To the major)* How's Mary getting on with the Nugget, major?

Major. Well enough for her, I fancy.   As for him ——

Lady Mary (from the sofa). And so you believe in first love, Sir Thomas? Ha! ha!

Sir Thomas (gravely). I do, Lady Mary.

Lady Mary. And that a man never forgets her?

Sir Thomas. Perhaps.

Lady Mary. Ha! ha! ha! Gilda, Plumtre, look here! see what I've discovered! Here's—ha! ha! ha! *(pointing to Edgecomb)*—here's a sentimentalist, in London!

(All laugh.   Plumtre looks quickly at Edgecomb, who returns the gaze.   The major watches both.   Curtain.)

ACT III.

SCENE I.—*Morning-room in Mr. Welters's house.* LADY MARY *alone.*

Lady Mary. And so this is the day! *(Walks to the window and looks out.)* It looked strange and terrible this morning at dawn; it looks vulgar and commonplace at high noonday. The city was mysterious and awful then; it is cheap enough now. And I am in my heyday, they tell me. A London dawn, and a London noon. What made that man Edgecomb stick by me so last night, I wonder? And where was Welters? At the Club, I suppose—drunk, or worse. He has not returned home yet, my lord and master. Edgecomb—Edgecomb. Let me see: Sir Thomas Edgecomb. He brought me home at dawn. It was a caprice, I suppose. But, after all, Welters was away; and he was less scandalous than Plumtre would have been. This is the last day it will make much difference, I suppose. Edgecomb—Edgecomb; something of him reminds me of the dawn again—my own, in London. *(Enter* LADY STRANGEWAYS.*)* Gilda, who's——

Lady Strangeways. Good-morning, Mary dear. You were radiant last night; and those superb diamonds!—they made me cry with envy.

Lady Mary. Tell me, Gilda, who's Edgecomb?

Lady Strangeways. Oh, I don't know; some rich Australian who tumbled from a third-cousinship into an Irish baronetcy just in the nick of time. Who gave you the diamonds, Molly? Not Welters? Some one said they were old family diamonds; and Welters hasn't any family, you know.

Lady Mary. How long have you known it, Gilda?

Lady Strangeways. Only since I was married, I grant you, Mary. We both married well, I confess— Welters the famous young London beauty, and I——

Lady Mary. And you the rich old *roué.*

Lady Strangeways. Just so!—your uncle. Ha! ha! ha! Come, Mary, let's be good-natured again. Upon my word, dear, I hope you and Plum won't go too far; London would be quite too awfully slow without you. But, seriously, Mary, what can we get up next? Everybody's talking about Mrs. Mayfly and her odious charity ball. I hear the Prince has been there three times already. But first just tell me who gave you those diamonds. Trappington swore he saw the Plumtre crest upon a locket. Welters can't have done it; he's quite pumped dry, I hear. Besides, no man gives such diamonds to his wife nowadays— now that ——

Lady Mary. Now that you and I set the fashion.

Lady Strangeways. Just so, my dear. Oh, you can't offend me; it's no use, you know. Even Strangeways can't.

Lady Mary. Gilda, who was the Nugget? His name wasn't always Edgecomb?

Lady Strangeways. Oh, no; some nobody; he never would have taken you home in your carriage in those days, Mary.   But he went to Australia, and came back all new-gilt.   Let's see; what was the man's name?   Something like a beast, or brute, I know. Stop—yes—Bruton, that was it.

Lady Mary. Tom Bruton !

Lady Strangeways. Where's Plumtre?

Lady Mary. I don't know.

Lady Strangeways. There he comes.   Talk of the —person with Faust, you know——   Good-bye, Mary—Margherita; can't stop to play Dame Martha, you know, ha! ha! ha!   Oh, just one word first, though.   *(To Plumtre, at the door)* Stay out, you naughty fellow.   You can't come in now.   *(To Lady Mary)* Mary dear, do think what we can do against that Mayfly woman; she's making terrible running, you know, even as the *inconnue, ingénue,* or what not.   As soon as she gets clever enough to be fast, it's all up with us, my dear—mark my words, it's all up.   Good-bye.   Ta ta, Plum.   *(Kisses her hand to Plumtre, and exit.)*

Plumtre. Gay creature, Lady Strangeways; such good company.   *(Stands until she is well out of sight, then seats himself.)*   All is ready, dearest; we leave Mrs. Mayfly's at midnight, drive around the town, and catch the tidal express.

Lady Mary (rises impatiently).   And, pray, suppose I do not choose to accompany you?

Plumtre. But you will not! but you cannot!   Think

a moment; it is impossible to draw back now, Lady Mary.

Lady Mary. Impossible? Earl Plumtre does himself too much honor.

Plumtre. Do you not love me, Mary? I, who adore you! — I, who worship the very ground you tread upon! — I, who — who have promised to marry you as soon as — as soon as ——

Lady Mary. A noble ambition, indeed, to marry your lordship!

(Starts as if to leave the room. A footman enters with a letter. Lady Mary tears it open and reads to herself.)

"Shall not return at present. Try and send me some money by the bearer; if there is none in the house borrow of Strangeways — or Plumtre." *(Crumples up the letter and lets it fall. To the footman)* Tell your master there is no answer.

Plumtre. And to-night?

Lady Mary. I — I will see you at Mrs. Mayfly's. *(Exit.)*

Plumtre (alone). So. She will see me at Mrs. Mayfly's. *(Rises and walks about nervously.)* I wonder am I making a damned fool of myself? *(Sits down again and drums on the table.)* Well, after all, I'm not the only one.

(Rises and walks to the door. Enter EDGECOMB.)

Edgecomb. Good-morning, Lord Plumtre.

Plumtre (carelessly). Good-day, sir. Ah! you wish to see Lady Mary?

Edgecomb. Not particularly.

Plumtre. Lady Mary is not at home, sir.

Edgecomb. I can wait. *(Seats himself.)*

Plumtre (angrily). Lady Mary is not receiving, sir.

Edgecomb. You will do quite as well.

Plumtre (furiously). I have not the pleasure of your acquaintance, sir.

Edgecomb. Oh, yes, you have. I have known you for some time. I have been meaning for several months to say a word to you, and this seems to be a fitting occasion. You must discontinue your dishonorable attentions to Lady Mary, and ——

Plumtre (during the first of Edgecomb's speech seems dumb with astonishment ; then interrupts in a burst of anger. I? Lady Mary? You are mad! you — you are a liar, sir! you — you ——

Edgecomb (continuing). And then leave London. Perhaps you had better leave London at once. I—I should advise it.

Plumtre (making a violent effort to master himself). And—and who may you be? And—and by what right do you presume ——

Edgecomb. I am a friend of Lady Mary's.

Plumtre. Indeed! I—I shall ask her for a reference. I—I had thought you were a' gambler, a—a common blackleg, sir; a ——

Edgecomb. You will do wisely not to repeat your remark, Lord Plumtre, but to follow my advice.

Plumtre. And, pray, suppose I do not choose to do so?

Edgecomb. I shall appeal to Lady Mary herself.

Plumtre. And suppose she has you shown the door — as I should do, did you dare to say this in my own house?

Edgecomb. I should make you do so.

Plumtre (tries to laugh). Fortunately, sir, your power is not equal to your presumption.

Edgecomb. My power is in my right — the right of any honorable man to stop a shameful wrong.

(Enter LADY MARY.*)*

Lady Mary. Good-morning, Sir Thomas.

Plumtre. This — this person has forced himself upon you, Lady Mary. I told him you were not at home, but he ——

Lady Mary. I am always at home to my friends, Sir Thomas. I shall hope to see you to-night, Lord Plumtre.

(Exit Plumtre. Lady Mary beckons Edgecomb to a chair.)

It is kind of you to call so soon, Sir Thomas. I was thinking of you only this morning, and of the message that you told me you had for me.

Edgecomb. It is but a sad errand, Lady Mary — a message from beyond the grave. I hardly know how to begin. I do not know how he would have me begin.

(Lady Mary takes a seat and looks at him curiously. Edgecomb remains standing, his eyes fixed upon the ground.)

Lady Mary. Pray, whom do you mean?

Edgecomb. Whom? I do not know. I fear you have forgotten him. And yet you loved him once. Oh, Mary, — Mary Maberly, — what are you doing?

Do you know what you are doing? Look at me; I am Tom Bruton. Do you remember me now? Do you remember him? Do you remember that evening at Shropshire House—and the rose you gave him?

Lady Mary. Do I remember him?

Edgecomb. Arthur Gordon. You loved him once.

Lady Mary. I loved him once! Did I ever love any one? *(Musingly)* I fancy not; I gave it up—all that. Arthur Gordon—— *(A pause. Edgecomb raises his eyes to her; she looks down again.)* Where is he?

Edgecomb. He is dead.

Lady Mary. Was this your message?

Edgecomb. He died with me, in Australia. Before he died he bade me see you once and give you back —this. *(Edgecomb draws from his breast a withered rose, and places it in her hands. A long pause.)* You remember, now?

Lady Mary. I remember what? I remember Arthur Gordon. *(Eagerly)* Did he love me much, you say?

Edgecomb. He loved you with his life.

Lady Mary. And he is dead. *(Rising)* Pray, Sir Thomas, is this all?

Edgecomb. But a word more. Lady Mary, by your memory of Arthur, I entreat you—of Arthur, whom, alone, we both loved—— Ah, how can I say it? I saw Lord Plumtre here just now——

Lady Mary. You presume too far, sir. *(Exit.)*

Edgecomb. What can I do?

(Enter Welters.*)*

Welters. Ha, Edgecomb, good-morning.

Edgecomb. Good-morning. I must go.

Welters. Say, Edgecomb, stop a moment; those shares of yours are turning out a good thing, eh? It was kind of you to put me up to them. Tell me, is it time to sell yet?

Edgecomb. No, no; don't sell. Good-bye. *(Exit.)*

Welters. Now, what's he in such a devil of a hurry for? I wonder has he seen her ladyship?

SCENE II.—*The entrance-ball at Mrs. Mayfly's. A stone stair-case in the back-ground. Visitors passing up the stairs and entering; an orchestra beard in the distance. Enter* TRAP-PINGTON. *He bows to* MRS. MAYFLY.

Mrs. Mayfly. So kind of you to come, duke! Is her Grace with you?

Duke. The duchess is indisposed, dear lady.

Mrs. Mayfly. I am so sorry.

(Enter LADY MARY WELTERS, *with* PLUMTRE.*)*

How do you do, dear Lady Mary? Is Mr. Welters with you?

Lady Mary. No. I wish to present Lord Plumtre.

(Pantomime of introduction. Plumtre forgets to bow, but stares at EDGECOMB *approaching. Exeunt Trappington and Mrs. Mayfly; Edgecomb with Lady Mary. Enter* MAJOR BRANDYBALL.*)*

Plumtre. Now, damn his insolence!

Major. Whose insolence, Plumtre?

Plumtre. That infernal Edgecomb. Brandyball, I'll kill that man.

Major. You can't, Plum. Duelling's bad form, you know.

Plumtre. Then I'll thrash him !

Major. You can't, my lord ; he's too big.

(Enter LADY STRANGEWAYS.*)*

Lady Strangeways. Halloo, Plum ! What's this swearing I hear? You look glum, disconsolate. Where's Mary? Take me in to the Mayfly — there's a good fellow ; then I'll let you off; 'pon honor I will.

(Exeunt. Reënter EDGECOMB, *alone.)*

Major. Halloo, Tom ! look here. I want a word with you. *(Draws him aside.)* Have you had your revenge yet, Tom?

Edgecomb. No ; not yet.

Major. I am afraid, my poor boy, you won't be needed. It will go all of itself, as the French say. Plumtre will take care of that, or I'm much mistaken. I'm sorry — for poor Arthur.

Edgecomb (sadly.) Poor Arthur!

Major. As for you, I don't wholly admire your later self, Tom Bruton, if it's the true one.

Edgecomb. Arthur Gordon was my other self; and I sometimes fear it went with him. *(They pause. Lady Mary passes with Plumtre. Edgecomb, looking after her, to himself)* And that was Mary Maberly !

Major. She doesn't look well to-night. She looks pale.

Edgecomb. I must try once more. *(Exit.)*

Major. Poor fellow! what can he do, against all those diamonds, and Welters into the bargain?

(Enter PLUMTRE, meeting Edgecomb as he goes out.)

Plumtre. Ah, our friend the Nugget again.   Pray, sir, you appealed from me to Lady Mary this morning; may I venture to ask with what result?

Edgecomb. Leave the house, sir! leave the house, or, by God, I will make of you a sport for the town!

Plumtre. This is a lady's house, sir; you do not have them in the bush. *(Exeunt.)*

Major. Humph! there will be trouble, I see that; there will be trouble.

(Enter a footman.)

Footman. Lord Plumtre's carriage.

(Reênter EDGECOMB.)

Edgecomb. Major, have you seen her? She has not gone?

Major. She has not gone. I shall be here some time, Edgecomb. *(Exit Edgecomb.   Major Brandyball, to himself)* Can we stop it? Better anything than — than —— By heavens, here she comes!

(Enter LADY MARY, with PLUMTRE. The orchestra plays loudly in the distance.)

Plumtre. Call Lord Plumtre's carriage.
Footman. It is here, your lordship.

(Plumtre goes to the door and looks out. Enter EDGECOMB.)

Edgecomb (loudly). Call Lady Mary Welters's carriage.   Lady Mary, will you take my arm?

(Lady Mary takes Edgecomb's arm, as if at his command. Plumtre returns.)

Plumtre. Lady Mary is with me, sir.

Edgecomb. Out of my way, sir!

Plumtre. I tell you, sir, Lady Mary is with me.

(He presses forward rudely; Edgecomb strikes Plumtre in the face with his left arm, his right in Lady Mary's. Plumtre is hurled backwards down the stairs, and falls motionless upon the marble floor. Lady Mary turns pale, but makes no sound).

Major. By heaven, he has it!

Edgecomb. Now, Lady Mary, come with me.

(Lady Mary is led away by him as if spell-bound. Exeunt.)

Major (to the servants). A hundred guineas apiece, my men, to keep this quiet.

Footman (at the lower door, touching his hat). What shall we do with him, sir? *(pointing to Plumtre, who is lying motionless).*

Major. Carry him to his lodgings.

Footman. I'm afraid he's 'most done for, sir.

(They lift Plumtre, and carry him out heavily upon their shoulders.)

Lady Strangeways (speaking from above). Have you seen Mary, Major Brandyball?

Major. She has just gone home, Lady Strangeways.

SCENE III.—*Mr. Welters's house, as before.* LADY MARY *on a sofa, weeping;* EDGECOMB *by her side.*

Edgecomb. I must go now, Lady Mary; I must say good-bye. I am glad if I have been of service to you; but I have kept my promise to Arthur, and must go.

Lady Mary (sobbing). Oh, do not go; do not go yet. Save me from him. I cannot look to Mr. Welters. I cannot dare to be alone again.

Edgecomb. I have saved you from yourself; he cannot harm you. Welters will take you abroad to-morrow.

Lady Mary. And you?

Edgecomb. I go back to Australia.

Lady Mary (grasping his hand). Oh, do not go! do not leave me! Stay here, near me, always.

Edgecomb. I cannot.

Lady Mary. See; I have not forgotten. It is you who will have forgotten, if you go. I remember all now. But you were two then. Do you not remember? You, too, loved me once. You do not —you cannot have forgotten?

Edgecomb. I remember Arthur. And I could not bear to think, though he were dead, that he might know. For Arthur's sake I came—not for mine.

Lady Mary. But you loved me, then? You have not forgotten?

Edgecomb (at the door). I have forgotten. Arthur is dead. It is only Arthur who has not forgotten.

July.

Our Consul at Carlsruhe.

BEING A MIDDLE-AGED LIFE'S DREAM.

IED.—*In Baden, Germany, the 22d instant, Charles Austin Pinckney, late U. S. Consul at Carlsruhe, aged sixty years.*

There: most stories of men's lives end with the epitaph, but this of Pinckney's shall begin there. If we, as haply God or Devil can, could unroof the houses of men's souls,—if their visible works were of their hearts rather than their brains,—we should know strange things. And this alone, of all the possible, is certain. For bethink you, how men appear to their Creator, as he looks down into the soul, that matrix of their visible lives we find so hard to localize and yet so sure to be. For all of us believe in self, and few of us but are forced, one way or another, to grant existence to some selves outside of us. Can you not fancy that men's souls, like their farms, would show here a patch of grain, and there the tares; there the weeds and here the sowing; over this place the rain has been, and that other, to one looking down upon it from afar, seems brown and desolate, wasted by

159

fire or made arid by the drouth? In this man's life
is a poor beginning, but a better end; in this other's
we see the foundations, the staging, and the schemes
of mighty structures, now stopped, given over, or
abandoned; of vessels, fashioned for the world's seas,
now rotting on the stocks. Of this one all seems
ready but the launching; of that the large keelson
only has been laid; but both alike have died unborn,
and the rain falls upon them, and the mosses grow:
the sound of labor is far off, and the scene of work is
silent. Small laws make great changes; slight differ-
ences of adjustment end quick in death. Small, now,
they would seem to us; but to the infinite mind all
things small and great are alike; the spore of rust in
the ear is very slight, but a famine in the corn will
shake the world.

Pinckney's life the world called lazy; his leisure
was not fruitful, and his sixty years of life were but
a gentleman's. Some slight lesion may have caused
paralysis of energy, some clot of heart's blood pressed
upon the soul: I make no doubt our doctors could
diagnose it, if they knew a little more. Tall and
slender, he had a strange face, a face with a young
man's beauty; his white hair gave a charm to the
rare smile, like new snow to the Spring, and the
slight stoop with which he walked was but a grace
the more. In short, Pinckney was interesting.
Women raved about him; young men fell in
love with him; and if he was selfish, the fault
lay between him and his Maker, not visible to

other men. There are three things that make a man interesting in his old age : the first, being heroism, we may put aside ; but the other two are regret and remorse. Now, Mr. Pinckney's fragrance was not of remorse—women and young men would have called it heroism : it may have been. As much heroism as could be practiced in thirty-six years of Carlsruhe.

Why Carlsruhe? That was the keynote of inquiry; and no one knew. Old men spoke unctuously of youthful scandals ; women dreamed. I suspect even Mrs. Pinckney wondered, about as much as the plowed field may wonder at the silence of the autumn. But Pinckney limped gracefully about the sleepy avenues which converge at the Grand Duke's palace, like a wakeful page in the castle of the Sleeping Beauty. Pinckney was a friend of the Grand Duke's, and perhaps it was a certain American flavor persisting in his manners which made him seem the only man at the Baden court who met his arch-serene altitude on equal terms. For one who had done nothing and possessed little, Pinckney certainly preserved a marvelous personal dignity. His four daughters were all married to scions of Teutonic nobility ; and each one in turn had asked him for the Pinckney arms, and quartered them into the appropriate check-square with as much grave satisfaction as he felt for the far-off patch of Hohenzollern, or of Hapsburg in sinister chief. Pinckney had laughed at it and referred them to the Declaration of Independence, clause the first; but his wife had copied them from some spoon or sugar-bowl. She was very fond of Pinckney, and no more questioned him why they always lived in Carlsruhe than a Persian would the sun for rising east. Now and then they went to Baden, and her cup was full.

Pinckney died of a cold, unostentatiously, and was buried like a gentleman; though the Grand Duke actually wanted to put the court in mourning for three days, and consulted with his chamberlain whether it would do. Mrs. Pinckney had preceded him by some six years; but she was an appendage, and her husband's deference had always seemed in Carlsruhe a trifle strained. It was only in these last six years that any one had gossiped of remorse, in answer to the sphinx-like question of his marble brow. Such questions vex the curious. Furrows trouble nobody—money matters are enough for them; but white smoothness in old age is a bait, and tickles curiosity. Some said, at home he was a devil, and beat his wife.

But Pinckney never beat his wife. Late in the last twilight of her life she had called him to her, and excluded even the four daughters, with their stout and splendid barons; then, alone with him, she looked to him and smiled. And suddenly his gentleman's heart took a jump, and the tears fell on her still soft hands. I suppose some old road was opened again in the gray matter of his brain. Mrs. Pinckney smiled the more strongly and said — not quite so terribly as Mrs. Amos Barton : "Have I made you happy, dearest Charles ?" And Charles, the perfect-mannered, said she had ; but said it stammering. "Then," said she, "I die very happily, dear." And she did ; and Pinckney continued to live at Carlsruhe.

The only activities of Pinckney's mind were critical. He was a wonderful orator, but he rarely spoke. People said he could have been a great writer, but he never wrote, at least, nothing original. He was the art and continental-drama critic of several English and American reviews ; in music, he was a Wagnerian, which debarred him from writing of it except in German ; but the little Court Theatre at Carlsruhe has Wagner's portrait over the drop-curtain, and the consul's box was never empty when the mighty heathen legends were declaimed or the holy music of the Grail was sung. In fiction of the earnest sort, and poetry, Pinckney's critical pen showed a marvelous magic, striking the scant springs of the author's inspiration through the most rocky ground of incident or style. He had a curious sympathy with youthful tenderness. But, after all, as every young compatriot who went to Baden said, what the deuce and all did he live in Baden for ? Miles Breeze had said it in 'Fifty, when he made the grand tour with his young wife, and dined with him in Baden-Baden ; that is, when Breeze dined with him, for his young wife was indisposed and could not go. Miles Breeze, junior, had said it, as late as 'Seventy-six, when he went abroad, ostensibly for instruction, after leaving col-

lege. He had letters to Mr. Pinckney, who was very
kind to the young Baltimorean, and greatly troubled
the Grand Duke his Serenity, by presenting him as a
relative of the Bonapartes. Many another American
had said it, and even some leading politicians : he
might have held office at home : but Pinckney continued to live in Carlsruhe.

His critical faculties seemed sharpened, after his
wife's death, as his hair grew whiter ; and if you
remember how he looked before, you must have
noticed that the greatest change was in the expression
of his face. There was one faint downward line at
either side of his mouth, and the counterpart at the
eyes ; a doubtful line which, faint as it was graven,
gave a strange amount of shading to the face. And
in speaking of him still earlier, you must remember
to take your india-rubber and rub out this line from
his face. This done, the face is still serious ; but it
has a certain light, a certain air of confidence, of
determination, regretful though it be, which makes
it loved by women. Women can love a desperate,
but never begin to love a beaten cause. Women fell
in love with Pinckney, for the lightning does strike
twice in the same place ; but his race was rather that
of Lohengrin than of the Asra, and he saw it, or seemed
to see it, not. Still, in these times those downward
lines had not come, and there was a certain sober
light in his face as of a sorrowful triumph. This
was in the epoch of his greatest interestingness to
women.

When he first came to Carlsruhe, he was simply the new consul, nothing more; a handsome young man, almost in his honeymoon, with a young and pretty wife. He had less presence in those days, and seemed absorbed in his new home, or deeply sunk in something; people at first fancied he was a poet, meditating a great work, which finished, he would soon leave Carlsruhe. He never was seen to look at a woman, not overmuch at his wife, and was not yet popular in society.

But it was true that he was newly married. He was married in Boston, in 'Forty-three or four, to Emily Austin, a far-off cousin of his, whom he had known (he himself was a Carolinian) during his four years at Cambridge. For his four years in Cambridge were succeeded by two more at the Law School; then he won a great case against Mr. Choate, and was narrowly beaten in an election for Congress; after that it surprised no one to hear the announcement of his engagement to Miss Austin, for his family was unexceptionable and he had a brilliant future. The marriage came in the fall, rather sooner than people expected, at King's Chapel. They went abroad, as was natural; and then he surprised his friends and hers by accepting his consulship and staying there. And they were imperceptibly, gradually, slowly, and utterly forgotten.

The engagement came out in the spring of 'Forty-three. And in June of that year young Pinckney had gone to visit his *fiancée* at Newport. Had you seen him there, you would have seen him in perhaps the brightest rôle that fate has yet permitted on this world's stage.   A young man, a lover, rich, gifted, and ambitious, of social position unquestioned in South Carolina and the old Bay State — all the world loved him, as a lover ; the many envied him, the upper few desired him. ∙ Handsome he has always remained.

And the world did look to him as bright as he to the world.   He was in love, as he told himself, and Miss Austin was a lovable girl ; and the other things he was dimly conscious of ; and he had a long vacation ahead of him, and was to be married late in the autumn, and he walked up from the wharf in Newport, swinging his cane, and thinking on these pleasant things.

Newport, in those days, was not the paradise of cottages and curricles, of lawns and laces, of new New-Yorkers and Nevada miners ; it was the time of big hotels and balls, of Southern planters, of Jullien's orchestras, and of hotel hops ; such a barbarous time as the wandering New-Yorker still may find, lingering on the simple shores of Maine, sunning in the verdant valleys of the Green Mountains ; in short, it was Arcadia, not Belgravia.   And you must remember that Pinckney, who was dressed in the latest style, wore a blue broadcloth frock-coat, cut very low and tight in the waist, with a coat-collar rolling back to reveal a vast expanse of shirt-bosom, surmounted by a cravat of awful splendor, bow-knotted and blue-fringed. His trousers were of white duck, his boots lacquered, and he carried a gold-tipped cane in his hand. So he walked up the narrow old streets from the wharf, making a sunshine in those shady places. It was the hottest hour of a midsummer afternoon; not a soul was stirring, and Pinckney was left to his own pleasant meditations.

He got up the hill and turned into the park by the old mill; over opposite was the great hotel, its piazzas deserted, silent even to the hotel band. But one flutter of a white dress he saw beneath the trees, and then it disappeared behind them, causing Pinckney to quicken his steps. He thought he knew the shape and motion, and he followed it until he came upon it suddenly, behind the trees, and it turned.

A young girl of wonderful beauty, rare, erect carriage, and eyes of a strange, violet-gray, full of much meaning. This was all Pinckney had time to note; it was no one he had ever seen before. He had gone up like a hunter, sure of his game, and too far in it to retract. The embarrassment of the situation was such that Pinckney forgot all his cleverness of manner, and blurted out the truth like any school-boy.

"I beg pardon — I was looking for Miss Austin," said he; and he raised his hat.

A delightful smile of merriment curled the beauty's lips. "My acquaintance with Miss Austin is too slight to justify my finding her for you; but I wish you all success in your efforts," she said, and vanished, leaving the promising young lawyer to blush at his own awkwardness and wonder who she was. As she disappeared, he only saw that her hair was a lustrous coil of pale gold-brown, borne proudly.

He soon found Emily Austin, and forgot the beauty, as he gave his betrothed a kiss and saw her color heighten; and in the afternoon they took a long drive. It was only at tea, as he was sitting at table with the Austins in the long dining-room, that some one walked in like a goddess; and it was she. He asked her name; and they told him it was a Miss Warfield, of Baltimore, and she was engaged to a Mr. Breeze.

In the evening there was a ball; and as they were dancing (for every one danced in those days) he saw her again, sitting alone this time and unattended. She was looking eagerly across the room, through the dancers and beyond; and in her eyes was the deepest look of sadness Pinckney had ever seen in a girl's face; a look such as he had thought no girl could feel. A moment after, and it was gone, as some one spoke to her; and Pinckney wondered if he had not been mistaken, so fleeting was it, and so strange. An acquaintance — one of those men who delight to act as brokers of acquaintances — who had noticed his gaze came up. "That is the famous Miss Mary Warfield," said he. "Shall I not introduce you?"

"No," said Pinckney; and he turned away rudely. To be rude when you like is perhaps one of the choicest prerogatives of a good social position. The acquaintance stared after him, as he went back to

Miss Austin, and then went up and spoke to Miss Warfield himself. A moment after, Pinckney saw her look over at him with some interest; and he wondered if the man had been ass enough to tell her. Pinckney was sitting with Emily Austin; and, after another moment, he saw Miss Warfield look at her. Then her glance seemed to lose its interest; her eyelids drooped, and Pinckney could see, from her interlocutor's manner, that he was put to his trumps to keep her attention. At last he got away, awkwardly; and for many minutes the strange girl sat like a statue, her long lashes just veiling her eyes, so that Pinckney, from a distance, could not see what was in them. Suddenly the veil was drawn and her eyes shone full upon him, her look meeting his. Pinckney's glance fell, and his cheeks grew redder. Miss Warfield's face did not change, but she rose and walked, though unattended, through the centre of the ball-room to the door. Pinckney's seat was nearer it than hers; she passed him as if without seeing him, moving with unconscious grace, though it would not have been the custom at that time for a girl to cross so large a room alone. Just then some one asked Miss Austin for a dance; and Pinckney, who was growing weary of it, went out on the piazza for a cigar, and then, attracted by the beauty of the night, strayed further than he knew, alone, along the cliffs above the sea.

The next day he was walking with Miss Austin, and they passed her, in her riding habit, waiting by the mounting-stone ; she bowed to Miss Austin alone, leaving him out, as it seemed to Pinckney, with exaggerated care.

" Is she not beautiful ? " said Emily, ardently.

" Humph ! " said Pinckney. A short time after, as they were driving on the road to the Fort, he saw her again ; she was riding alone, across country, through the rocky knolls and marshy pools that form the southern part of the Rhode Island.   She had no groom lagging behind, but it was not so necessary then as now ; and, indeed, a groom would have had a hard time to keep up with her, as she rattled up the granite slopes and down over logs and bushes with her bright bay horse.   The last Pinckney saw of her she disappeared over a rocky hill against the sky; her beautiful horse flecked with foam, quivering with happy animal life, and the girl calm as a figure carved in stone, with but the faintest touch of rose upon her face, as the pure profile was outlined one moment against the sunlit blue.

" How recklessly she rides ! " whispered Miss Austin to him, and Pinckney said *yes*, absently, and, whipping up his horse, drove on, pretending to listen to his fiancée's talk. It seemed to be about dresses, and rings, and a coming visit to the B——s, at Nahant. He had never seen a girl like her before ; she was a puzzle to him.

" It is a great pity she is engaged to Mr. Breeze," said Miss Austin ; and Pinckney woke up with a start, for he was thinking of Miss Warfield too.

" Why ? " said he.

"I don't like him," said Emily. "He isn't good enough for her."

As this is a thing that women say of all wooers after they have won, and which the winner is usually at that period the first to admit, Pinckney paid little attention to this remark. But that evening he met Miles Breeze, saw him, talked with him, and heard others talk of him. A handsome man, physically ; well made, well dressed, well fed ; well bred, as breeding goes in dogs or horses ; a good shot, a good sportsman, yachtsman, story-teller ; a good fellow, with a weak mouth; a man of good old Maryland blood, yet red and healthy, who had come there in his yacht and had his horses sent by sea. A well-appointed man, in short ; provided amply with the conveniences of fashionable life. A man of good family, good fortune, good health, good sense, good nature, whom it were hypercritical to charge with lack of soul. "The first duty of a gentleman is to be a good animal," and Miles Breeze performed it thoroughly. Pinckney liked him, and he could have been his companion for years and still have liked him, except as a husband for Miss Warfield.

He could not but recognize his excellence as a *parti*. But the race of Joan of Arc does not mate with Bonhomme Richard, even when he owns the next farm. Pinckney used to watch the crease of Breeze's neck, above the collar, and curse.

Coming upon Miss Austin, one morning, she had said, "Come—I want to introduce you to Miss Warfield." Pinckney had demurred, and offered as an excuse that he was smoking. " Nonsense, Charles,"said the girl ; "I have told her you are coming." Pinck ney threw away his cigar and followed, and the presentation was made. Miss Warfield drew herself almost unusually erect after courtesying, as if in pro-test at having to bow at all. She was so tall that, as Emily stood between them, he could meet Miss War-field's iron-gray eyes, above her head. It was the first time in Pinckney's life that he had consciously not known what to say.

"I was so anxious to have you meet Charles before he left," said Emily. Evidently, his fiancée had been expatiating upon him to this new friend, and if there is anything that puts a man in a foolish position, it is to have this sort of preamble precede an acquaintance.

"An anxiety I duly shared, Miss Warfield, I assure you," said he ; which was a truth spoiled in the uttering—what the conversational Frenchman terms *banale.*

"Thank you," said Miss Warfield, very simply and tremendously effectively. Pinckney, for the second time with this young lady, felt himself a school-boy. Emily interposed some feeble common-places, and then, after a moment, Miss Warfield said, "I must go for my ride"; and she left, with a smile for Emily and the faintest possible glance for him. She went off with Breeze ; and it gave Pinckney some relief to see that she seemed equally to ignore the presence of the man who was her acknowledged lover, as he trotted on a small smart cob beside her. That evening, when he went on the piazza after tea, he found her sitting alone, in one corner, with her hands folded : it was one peculiarity about this woman that she was never seen with work. She made no sign of recognition as he approached ; but, none the less, he took the chair that was beside her and waited a moment for her to speak. " Have you found Miss Austin ? " said the beauty, with the faintest trace of malice in her coldly modulated tones, not looking at him. " I am not looking for Miss Austin," said he ; and she continued not looking at him, and so this strange pair sat there in the twilight, silent.

What was said between them I do not know. But in some way or other their minds met ; for long after Miss Austin and her mother had returned from some call, long after they had all left him, Pinckney continued to pace up and down, restlessly, in the dark. Pinckney had never seen a woman like this. After all, he was very young ; and he had, in his heart, supposed that the doubts and delights of his soul were peculiar to men alone. He thought all women — at all events, all young and worthy women — regarded life and its accepted forms as an accomplished fact, not to be questioned, and, indeed, too delightful to need it. The young South Carolinian, in his ambitions, in his heart-longings and heart-sickenings, in his poetry, even in his emotions, had always been lonely ; so that this loneliness had grown to seem to him as merely part of the day's work. The best women, he knew, were the best house-wives ; they were a rest and a benefit for the war-weary man, much as might be a pretty child, a bed of flowers, a strain of music.   With Emily Austin he should find all this ; and he loved her as good, pretty, amiable, perfect in her way.   But now, with Miss Warfield — it had seemed that he was not even lonely.

Pinckney did not see her again for a week.   When he met her, he avoided her ; she certainly avoided him.   Breeze, meantime, gave a dinner.   He gave it on his yacht, and gave it to men alone.   Pinckney was of the number.

The next day there was a driving party ; it was to drive out of town to Purgatory, a pretty place, where there is a brook in a deep ravine with a verdant meadow-floor ; and there they were to take food and drink, as is the way of humanity in pretty places. Now it so happened that the Austins, Miss War-field, Breeze, and Pinckney were going to drive in a party, the Austins and Miss Warfield having carriages of their own ; but at the last moment Breeze did not appear, and Emily Austin was incapacitated by a headache.   She insisted, as is the way of loving women, that " Charles should not lose it " ; for to her it was one of life's pleasures, and such pleasures satisfied her soul.   (It may be that she gave more of her soul to life's duties than did Charles, and life's pleasures were thus adequate to the remainder ; I do not know.)   Probably Miles Breeze also had a head-ache ; at all events, he did not, at the last moment, appear. It was supposable that he would turn up at the picnic; Mrs. Austin joined her daughter's entreaty; Miss Warfield was left unattended; in fine, Pinckney went with her.

Miss Warfield had a solid little phaeton with two stout ponies: she drove herself. For some time they were silent; then, insensibly, Pinckney began to talk and she to answer. What they said I need not say —indeed I could not, for Pinckney was a poet, a man of rare intellect and imagination, and Miss Warfield was a woman of this world and the next; a woman who used conventions as another might use a fan, to screen her from fools; whose views were based on the ultimate. But they talked of the world, and of life in it; and when it came to an end, Pinckney noted to himself this strange thing, that they had both talked as of an intellectual problem, no longer concerning their emotions—in short, as if this life were at an end, and they two were dead people discussing it.

So they arrived at the picnic, silent; and the people assembled looked to one another and smiled, and said to one another how glum those two engaged people looked, being together, and each wanting another. Mr. Breeze had not yet come; and as the people scattered while the luncheon was being prepared, Pinckney and she wandered off like the others. They went some distance—perhaps a mile or more— aimlessly; and then, as they seemed to have come about to the end of the valley, Pinckney sat down upon a rock, but she did not do so, but remained standing. Hardly a word had so far been said between them; and then Pinckney looked at her and said:

"Why are you going to marry Mr. Breeze?"

"Why not?"—listlessly.

"You might as well throw yourself into the sea," said Pinckney; and he looked at the sea which lay beyond them shimmering.

"That I had not thought of," said she; and she looked at the sea herself with more interest. Pinckney drew a long breath.

"But why this man?" he said at length.

"Why that man?" said the woman; and her beautiful lip curled, with the humor of the mind, while her eyes kept still the sadness of the heart, the look that he had seen in the ball-room. "We are all poor," she added; then scornfully, "it is my duty to marry."

"But Miles Breeze?" persisted Pinckney.

The lip curled almost to a laugh. "I never met a better fellow than Miles," said she; and the thought was so like his own of the night before that Pinckney gasped for breath. They went back, and had chicken-croquettes and champagne, and a band that was hidden in the wood made some wild Spanish music.

Going home, a curious thing happened. They had started first and far preceded all the others. Miss Warfield was driving; and when they were again in the main road, not more than a mile from the hotel,

Pinckney saw ahead of them, coming in a light trotting buggy of the sort that one associates with the gentry who call themselves "sports," two of the gentlemen whom he had met at Breeze's dinner the night before. Whether Miss Warfield also knew them he did not know; but they had evidently had more wine than was good for them, and were driving along in a reckless manner on the wrong side of the road. The buggy was much too narrow for the two; and the one that was driving leaned out towards them with a tipsy leer. Pinckney shouted at him, but Miss Warfield drove calmly on. He was on the point of grasping the reins, but a look of hers withheld him, and he sat still, wondering; and in a moment their small front wheel had crashed through both the axles and spider-web wheels of the trotting buggy. The shock of the second axle whirled them round, and Pinckney fell violently against the dasher, while Miss Warfield was thrown clear of the phaeton on the outer side. But she had kept the reins, and before Pinckney could get to her she was standing at her horses' heads, patting their necks calmly, with a slight cut in her forehead where she had fallen, and only her nostril quivering like theirs, as the horses stood there trembling. The buggy was a wreck, and the horse had disappeared; and the two men, sobered by the fall, came up humbly to her to apologize. She heard them silently, with a pale face like some injured queen's; and then, bowing to them their dismissal, motioned Pinckney into the phaeton, which, though much broken, was still standing, and, getting in herself, drove slowly home.

"She might have killed herself," thought Pinckney, but he held his peace, as if it were the most natural course of action in the world. To tell the truth, under the circumstances he might have done the same alone.

Then it began. Pinckney could not keep this woman out of his head. He would think of her at all times, alone and in company. Her face would come to him in the loneliness of the sea, in the loneliness of crowds; the strong spirit of the morning was hers, and the sadness of the sunset and the wakeful watches of the night. Her face was in the clouds of evening, in the sea-coal fire by night; her spirit in the dreams of summer morns, in the hopeless breakers on the stormy shores, in the useless, endless effort of the sea. Her eyes made some strange shining through his dreams; and he would wake, with a cry that she was going from him, in the deepest hours of the night, as if in the dreams he had lost her, vanishing forever in the daily crowd. Then he would lie awake until morning, and all the laws of God and men would seem like cobwebs to his sorrow, and the power of it freezing in his heart. This was the ultimate nature of his being, to follow her, as drop of water blends in drop of water, as frost rends rock. Let him then follow out his law, as other beings do theirs; gravitation has no conscience; should he be weaker than a drop of water, because he was conscious, and a man?

So these early morning battles would go on, and character, training, conscience, would go down before the simpler force, like bands of man's upon essential nature. Then, with the first ray of the dawn, he would think of Emily Austin, sleeping near him, perhaps dreaming of him, and his mad visions seemed to fade ; and he would rise, exhausted, and wander out among the fresh fields and green dewy lanes, and calm, contentful trees, and be glad that these things were so ; yet could these not be moved, nor their destiny be changed. And as for him, what did it matter?

So the days went by. And Emily Austin looked upon him with eyes of limitless love and trust, and Pinckney did not dare to look upon himself; but his mind judged by day-time and his heart strove by night. Hardly at all had he spoken to Miss Warfield since ; and no reference had ever been made between them to the accident, or to the talk between them in the valley. Only Pinckney knew that she was to be married very shortly ; and he had urged Miss Austin to hasten their own wedding.

Emily went off with her mother to pay her last visit among the family, and to make her preparations ; and it was deemed proper that at this time Pinckney should not be with her. So he stayed in Newport five long days, alone ; and during this time he never spoke to Miss Warfield. I believe he tried not to look at her : she did not look at him. And on the fifth night Pinckney swore that he must speak to her once more, whatever happened.

In the morning there was talk of a sailing party; and Pinckney noted Breeze busying himself about the arrangements. He waited; and at noon Breeze came to him and said that there was a scarcity of men: would he go? Yes. They had two sail-boats, and meant to land upon Conanicut, which was then a barren island without a house, upon the southern end, where it stretches out to sea.

Pinckney did not go in the same boat with Breeze and Miss Warfield; and, landing, he spent the afternoon with others and saw nothing of her. But after dinner was over, he spoke to her, inviting her to walk; and she came, silently. A strange evening promenade that was: they took a path close on the sheer brink of the cliffs, so narrow that one must go behind the other. Pinckney had thought at first she might be frightened, with the rough path, and the steepness of the rocks, and the breakers churning at their base; but he saw that she was walking erect and fearlessly. Finally she motioned him to let her go ahead; and she led the way, choosing indiscriminately the straightest path, whether on the verge of the sea or leading through green meadows. A few colorless remarks were made by him, and then he saw the folly of it, and they walked in silence. After nearly an hour, she stopped.

" We must be getting back," she said.

" Yes," said he, in the same tone ; and they turned, she still leading the way, while he followed silently.' They were walking toward the sunset;

the sun was going down in a bank of dense gray cloud, but its long, level rays came over to them, across a silent sea. She walked on, over the rugged cliff, like some siren, some genius of the place, with a sure, proud grace of step ; she never looked around, and his eyes were fixed upon the black line of her figure, as it went before him, toward the gray and blood-red sunset. It seemed to him this was the last hour of his life; and even as he thought, his ankle turned, and he stumbled and fell, walking unwittingly into one of the chasms, where the line of the cliff turned in. He grasped a knuckle of rock, and held his fall, just on the brink of a ledge above the sea. Miss Warfield had turned quickly and seen it all ; and she leaned down over the brink, with one hand around the rock and the other extended to help him, the ledge on which he lay being some six feet below. Pinckney grasped her hand and kissed it.

Her color did not change at this; but, with a strange strength in her beautiful lithe figure, she drew him up steadily, he helping partly with the other hand, until his knees rested on the path again. He stood up with some difficulty, as his ankle was badly wrenched.

"I am afraid you cannot walk," said she.

"Oh, yes," he answered ; and took a few steps to show her. The pain was great ; but she walked on, and he followed, as best he could, limping. She looked behind now, as if to encourage him ; and he set his teeth and smiled.

"We must not be late," she said. "It is growing dark, and they will miss us."

But they did not miss them; for when they got to the landing-place, both the sail-boats had left the shore without them. There was nothing but the purple cloud-light left by this time; but Pinckney fancied he could see her face grow pale, for the first time that day.

"We must get home," she said, hurriedly. "Is there no boat?"

Pinckney pointed to a small dory on the beach, and then to the sea. In the east was a black bank of cloud, rifted now and then by lightning; and from it the wind came down and the white caps curled angrily toward them.

"No matter," said she; "we must go."

Pinckney found a pair of oars under the boat, and dragged it, with much labor, over the pebbles, she helping him. The beach was steep and gravelly, with short breakers rather than surf; and he got the bow well into the water and held it there.

"Get in," said he.

Miss Warfield got into the stern, and Pinckney waded out, dragging the flat-bottomed boat until it was well afloat. Then he sprang in himself, and, grasping the oars, headed the boat for the Fort point across the channel, three miles away. She sat silently in the stern, and it was too dark for him to see her face. He rowed savagely.

But the wind was straight ahead, and the sea increasing every moment. They were not, of course, exposed to the full swell of the ocean ; but the wide sea-channel was full of short, fierce waves that struck the little skiff repeated rapid blows, and dashed the spray over both of them.

"Are you not afraid?" said he, calmly. "It is growing rougher every minute."

"Oh, no, Mr. Pinckney," said she. "Pray keep on."

Pinckney noticed a tremor of excitement in her voice ; but by a flash of lightning that came just then he saw her deep eyes fixed on his, and the pure white outline of her face undisturbed. So he rowed the harder, and she took a board there was and tried to steer ; and now and then, as the clouds were lit, he saw her, like a fleeting vision in the night.

But the storm grew stronger ; and Pinckney knew the boat that they were in was not really moving at all, though, of course, the swash of the waves went by and the drifted spray. He tried to row harder, but with the pain in his ankle and the labor he was nearly exhausted, and his heart jumped in his chest at each recover. "Can you not make it?" said she, in the dark ; and Pinckney vowed that he could, and set his teeth for a mighty pull. The oar broke, and the boat's head fell rapidly off in the trough of the sea. He quickly changed about his remaining oar, and with it kept the head to the wind.

"We must go back," he said, panting.

" I know," said she. The wind-storm was fairly
upon them ; and, in spite of all his efforts, an occasional wave would get upon the beam and spill its
frothing crest into the boat. Pinckney almost doubted
whether it would float until it reached the shore ; but
Miss Warfield did not seem in the least disturbed, and
spoke without a tremor in her voice. The lightning
had stopped now, and he could not see her.

He had miscalculated the force of the wind and
waves, however ; for in a very few minutes they
were driven broadside back upon the beach, almost
at the same place from which they had started. Miss
Warfield sprang out quickly, and he after, just as a
wave turned the dory bottom upward on the stones.

" They will soon send for us," he said ; and step-
ping painfully up the shore, he occupied himself with
spreading her shawl in a sheltered spot for them to
wait in. She sat down, and he beside her. He was
very wet, and she made him put some of the shawl
over himself. The quick summer storm had passed
now, with only a few big drops of rain ; and the
moon was breaking out fitfully, through veils of
driving clouds and their storm-scud. By its light he
looked at her, and their eyes met. Pinckney groaned
aloud, and stood up. " Would that they would never
come ; would God that we could — "

" We cannot," said she, softly, in a voice that he
had never heard from her before — a voice with tears
in it ; and the man threw himself down at her feet,
inarticulate, maddened. Then, with a great effort at

control, not touching her, but looking straight into her eyes, he said, in blunt, low speech : " Miss War-field, I love you — do you know it ? "

Her head sank slowly down ; but she answered, very low, but clearly, *yes.* Then their eyes met again ; and, by some common impulse, they rose and walked apart. After a few steps, he stopped, being lame, and leaned against the cliff; but she went on until her dark figure was blended with the shadows of the crags.

So, when the boat came back, its sail silvered by the moonlight, they saw it, and coming down, they met again ; but only as the party were landing on the beach. Several of the party had come back ; and Mr. Breeze, who was among them, was full of explanation how he had missed the first boat and barely caught the second, supposing that his fiancée was in the first. An awkward accident, but easily explained by Pinckney, with the strain in his ankle ; and, indeed, the others were too full of excuses for having forgotten them to inquire into the causes of their absence together.

Pinckney went to his room, and had a night of delirium. Toward morning, his troubled wakefulness ended, and he fell into a dream. He dreamed that in the centre of the world was one green bower, beneath a blossoming tree, and he and Miss Warfield were there. And the outer world was being destroyed, one sphere by fire and the other by flood, and there was only this bower left. But they could not stay there, or the tree would die. So they went away, he to the one side and she to the other, and the ruins of the world fell upon them, and they saw each other no more.

In the morning his delirium left him, and his will resumed its sway. He went down, and out into the green roads, and listened to the singing of the birds; and then out to the cliff-path, and there he found Miss Warfield sitting as if she knew that he would come. He watched her pure face while she spoke, and her gray eyes: the clear light of the morning was in them, and on the gleaming sea beyond.

"You must go," said she.

"Yes," he said, and that was all. He took her hand for one moment, and lifted it lightly to his lips; then he turned and took the path across the fields. When he got to the first stile, he looked around. She was still sitting there, turned toward him. He lifted his hat, and held it for a second or two; then he turned the corner of the hedge and went down to the town.

Thus it happened that this story, which began sadly, with an epitaph, may end with wedding bells:

MARRIED. *At King's Chapel, by the Rev. Dr. A——, the 21st of September, Charles Austin Pinckney to Emily, daughter of the late James Austin.*

August.

Gloriana: A Fairy Story.

WRITTEN IN AN AUGUST WOOD.

His is a funny story, but it is a very old story, very old indeed; so old that I should not venture to tell it, were it not for the very peculiar way in which it happened to Avice. It was Avice who thought it was very funny; and she came home with her large round eyes larger and rounder than I had ever seen them, except when her brother killed the kittens; and she told it to me thus, and I listened and believed, for I always believe a child, and what she sees in the forest.

Avice was walking along the high-road of a dusty country town, just where it ceased to be the high-road and became the Main street with a capital letter; there, as all of you know if you have ever been to Adams, is an iron truss bridge over a stream which smells nastily; and there also is a brick manufactory on the left, and a wooden manufacturing company on the right, and a row of mills down the dirty little ditch, hiding the railroad depot, which is just around the corner, with a hot track that smells of cinders, and goes with a jangling curve to Birdofreedomville. There is also a little shop, where a greasy Dutchman with a paunch sells rum and low spirits, but Avice did not know this, and thought of going in to buy one of the candy-balls in the window. All this was very wrong in Avice ; and, indeed, it was most improper and unconventional for a young lady to be so very far from home and ten miles from a governess, as any critic would take pains to show you if I did not say it here ; and, indeed, it is a great pity that so many newspapers' writers cannot be governesses or lord high chamberlains ; but no one of them was here to point out the impropriety of Avice's proceeding, or the extreme inappropriateness of a pretty little girl with a silk frock in a bar-room, except under the guidance of a Congregational preacher or a league of Ohio ladies. So Avice would unquestionably have entered to buy a candy bull's-eye had it not been for a horrid woman who came out and looked stupidly at Avice with bleared eyes. Her face was creased like the copper plate of an ocean chart ; she seemed to have come a long journey, and in her face, though sodden, too, and wrinkled, was a household edition of the "History of the World " — if you only knew enough to read between the lines. An old green shawl was thrown over her head ; she had a brown skirt, rent at the sides ; some dingy knit stuff wrapped about her body, but much torn, so that it showed a portion of her bosom, something like a ball dress, only that her neck was different in shape from a lady's, and much tanned. She stared vacantly at Avice, and attempted to ask some question; but Avice, who had been standing as if petrified, uttered a sharp cry and fled in much terror, disregarding the woman, who called after her that her name was Glory Ann, and begged Avice to return.

Just across the bridge the road began to go up hill, and Avice was so frightened that she ran through the village, hardly noticing the jeering remarks of a group of gentlemen who were standing (it being Sunday, and the shops closed) under a lamp-post, nor stopping to look at a Chinaman; and she ran only the faster when a smart boy set a bull-pup after her. The bull-pup barked very viciously, and attempted to bite her heels; but Avice continued to run, and the dog soon stopped when they got beyond the village, and there was no company present to "sick him" on and applaud his action.

Avice, however, ran several miles farther up the road, or lane — or perhaps some might call it a track (or even, to put a fine point upon it, a path)— which led into a thicket of white birches, not very big, through which Avice hurtled and fell in a hot little place, with long tussocks of grass, by the side of a rose anemone.

Now, I know some people might expect a long conversation between my heroine and the vegetable aforesaid; but Avice was a well-educated little girl who knew that the fairies are myths of the sun, a lump of coal a bottled sunbeam, and most things figures, down to God Almighty, who is a figure of speech. Judge, therefore, of Avice's surprise when, feeling thirsty and saying so, which was only part of her usual frankness, the anemone told her to try where the bee sucked, and, bending its head, showed her the source of a stream.

This was naturally a great surprise to Avice, who thought that all streams came from reservoirs or tanks; but here she found one clear globule of water, distilled on the root of the anemone; and this globule suddenly slid down into a dew-drop which was hanging on the under side of a blade of grass. It had been forgotten by the sun that morning, owing to the blade's having turned over in bed during the night; so the drop had not waked up in time, and was left behind. These two drops joined hands, and slid gayly down a long stem to the top of a rock with a wet face, where they met many companions; and Avice was so interested that she slid down after them, and fell into a spongy place, where these drops and a few million others were playing hide-and-go-seek amid the grasses. But it was a little girl who surprised Avice most, a baby lying, blue-eyed, among some ferns. Avice wondered very much who she was. She was dressed beautifully in gossamer long clothes, and Avice, having read English history, thought at first it might be the Princess of Wales, from the shape of the canopy of fern leaves that bent over her like the three feathers.

The baby was obviously too young to be provided with a card-case; so Avice looked to see if her clothing were marked, and sure enough, she found a yellow G stippled in the handkerchief with the dust of buttercups, and Avice jumped at once to the conclusion that her name must be Gentianella.

This was a very natural inference, seeing that there were only ten letters after the G, which was a given quantity, leaving, according to the well-known formula $\frac{n^n + n^{(n-1)} \cdots \cdots n}{n}$, only 164832724½ other possible interpretations, as Avice rapidly calculated; and she was feeling the glow which always, in a well-bred child, accompanies the scientific establishment of truth, when she observed that the baby was drinking up all the water of the stream. So "Good-bye," said she to Gentianella; and the child looked up at her and smiled.

But Avice went on to seek a lower fountain, and followed the little sinuous line of darker green that marked the water-course through the mountain grasses, until she came to a sort of ledge where the meadow ended and she could look over into a wood. Avice climbed down the ledge of rock on a grape-vine, and found herself in a long valley with a brown carpet of many years' leaves. The water, trickling in at the upper end, wound through it and tinkled out the other with a silvery clear cascade; the long trees waved their arms high up and caught little sparks of sunbeams, which they flung down upon the floor of the ravine, where a pretty little girl, just Avice's age, played butterfly-chase with them. The girl had a dress of rose-color and blue, as fine as Avice's, and this time Avice thought she would ask the name. But the dear little girl only ran along the valley, and, disappearing over the cascade (whose edge only Avice could just see as it curved over, rimmed with a sheen of sunlight), cried out something that sounded like Georgiana. However, Avice went on, and came out on a field, with her face to the sun and her back to the great purple mountain. Here the wood-choppers were at work, and a sweet smell came from the oblong piles of logs and the clean split pine. The brook was all covered over with a wattle of twigs; but Avice still managed to keep it until she climbed down another, but much more terrible cliff, into a deep gorge.

Here were wild and beautiful ferns, tempting scarlet berries, orchids, and golden trumpet-flowers, rich, mossy nooks amid the rocks, deep pools, and little bays of silver sand; but the sun still sifted through the stately hemlocks, and fell in flecks upon a young girl standing in a crystal basin, like Danaë amid her shower of gold. She stood with her white back to a waterfall, a place where a great rock jutted out in front of the cliff and the waterfall slipped modestly behind it, running softly over the moss, and only creamed into a churn of foam when it struck the black surface of the basin. And Avice thought the girl more beautiful than anything she had ever seen, and did not dare to ask her name, but only looked. But the fairy spoke: "Am I not queen?" she said; "then come."

And Avice walked on, and they came deep into the roots of the forest : strange, gray places, where it was never winter, never summer, and the night still lurked; huge cliffs, and crevices in the earth, netted from the sky with gnarled roots of trees, choked with the bodies of great rotting trunks, where spiders spun their webs across the whole ravine ; then through terrible descents, chasms where it was awful to look down; and as Avice climbed there, trembling, with pale face, the rush of water stunned her ears.

But at last they came to a silent spot, more beautiful than all the places Avice had seen on that strange day. A fringe of trees closed the end of a little lake, white with water-lilies ; the blue curtain of the mountains rose about and screened them from the world of men ; and Avice wished to stay there, playing with the flowers, till the sunset came, but still the fairy lady urged her on. Avice asked her name, and she turned as she reached the end of the lake, and waved her hand ; then she seemed to leap over, and one word, Gloriana, came back upon the wind.

Then Avice followed on to the end of the lake, and found it nothing but the wooden dam of a mill-pond ; and, climbing down, she found herself by a great heap of tan, in the yard of the mill. She knew that she had many miles yet to walk that day, or she would be late for dinner, and scolded by the governess, so she walked through the factory-yard, and was much surprised to find herself in the same road she had come by in the morning, close by the bridge ; and there was the same horrid old woman with the face like the copper plate ; only now she was walking in the bed of the dirty little canal, and the smart boy sat on a barrel shying stones at her bare feet, while the bull-pup looked on and growled.

The woman saw Avice, and turned. " How far is it to the sea ?" said she ; and, in turning, she seemed to have slipped upon a sharp stone, for she sank upon another, and Avice saw a little stream of blood upon her feet.   Avice would naturally make no reply to this, there being already much hurry, besides a horrid smell from the vent-gate of a dye-house opposite ; and she was wondering what had become of the fairy.   But the woman asked again earnestly ; and Avice said that it was about four inches on the map of the Eastern States in the school atlas.   At this the woman began to wring her hands, and Avice, to console her, said that the sea was but a horrid place with a smell of fish.   " Is it worse than this ?" the woman said, and Avice answered " Yes," encouragingly ; at least it was at Swampscott.   " Perhaps it won't be, farther out," said the woman, wearily ; and the last Avice saw of her she was trying to get up, and the dye in the stream had stained her white feet red and blue.

But Avice hurried home ; and, after she was punished for being late, she told to me this story, with her large round eyes.

September.

Passages from the Diary of a Hong-Kong Merchant.

TO BE READ IN THE SEASON, AT MOUNT DESERT.

ONG - KONG, June 14, 1882.—
This begins the fourteenth volume of my diary. Fourteen
volumes! I suspect that few
bachelors who have lived in one place, and passed
their lives in the China trade, can show so much.
And yet I, the journalist, in the days of my youth,
of my *jeunesse orageuse*, when I might have kept a
journal to some purpose, kept none at all. Perhaps
it is as well. It would not be pleasant reading now,
though it might serve as a lesson, which, however,
I hope I no longer need.

I am afraid there was not much of general interest
in volumes I. to XIII. inclusive. I doubt if even I
shall ever read them over. And I fear they will not
prove of absorbing interest to my heirs, remote collaterals as these must be. I kept my diary in order
to form systematic habits, and now that I have formed
the habits, they keep the diary. I wonder if this vol-

ume will be more interesting? Telegram to-day from
Rowbotham Brothers, ordering hemp, 800 barrels
first, June-July, 1881, x. on Bombay, deliverable all
October-December.

JUNE 15.—Telegraphed Rowbotham about his
hemp. Saw Russell to-day ; he is going home to get
married. Year after year 1 have seen my friends go
home to get married — some succeed and some of
them don't — leaving me in peace and Hong-Kong.
Many of them have gone, as the event proved, never
to return. . . . 1 wonder whether 1 shall ever go
home to get married? 1 suspect not. . . . Marriage
is one of those rash things we do in our youth.
Would 1 had never done anything worse !

JUNE 16.—Rowbotham by cable countermands
those two cargoes of hemp. 1 had already bought one
of them. This telegraphing has spoiled the China
trade. Now 1 have either got a lawsuit on my hands
or a cargo of hemp. Well, 1 prefer the hemp. 1 hate
rows, and would rather do anything than go to law.
A quiet life —   By-the-way, had a letter from Uncle
John to-day ; he wants me to go home and marry his
grandniece. Cabled, " Impossible to leave this year ;
fear a panic." Uncle John's mind must be going.

JUNE 17.— Saw Russell to-day. Never saw a man
so happy. He is going off Saturday. Told him of
my uncle's wanting me to go home. He slapped me
on my back (all the fellows slap me on the back —
luckily it is a stout one). " Rummy, my boy," said
he, " you must go with me." All the fellows call

me Rummy ; I don't know why ; I have never been intemperate in my habits. Didn't tell Russell why I was to go home. My uncle's grandniece, indeed ! She must be hardly out of long clothes. Why, her mother was hardly too old for me to be a little in love with her. I wonder if the daughter is like her ? Business very dull just now.

JUNE 18.— Cablegram from Uncle John : "Panic be damned ! Come at once. Don't break my heart." Just ten words. Intemperate old fellow, Uncle John. Of course I've got to go. He sent me out here, and now he sends me back. *Que la volonté de Uncle John soit faite*, as we say in French. A knowledge of French is the only profit I made, the last time I disobeyed Uncle John's orders. And now I am all he has got in the world ; that is, I and the grandniece. Russell seems delighted. Haven't told him about the grandniece, though ; it would never do. He would be certain to tell all the fellows ; and they insist on giving us a dinner the night before we go. Rowbotham took that hemp, after all ; very kind of him. Nice fellow, Rowbotham.

JUNE 19.— We had a great dinner last night. Very nice fellows these boys are in Hong-Kong, all of them. 'Pon my soul I was sorry to leave them, but said I'd be back in three or four months ; just the time to convince Uncle John of his folly, and I'll come home again to Hong-Kong. . . . Here we are on the steamer, already out of sight of land, and I'm smoking on the deck. Russell has a headache, and says, petulantly, he don't see how a fellow can do it. *I* don't see how a fellow can take too much wine on the very night that he is leaving Hong-Kong and going back to get married. If *I* were going home to get married, I am sure — After all, though, there's nearly ten years between us. He's a young fellow yet. His character isn't formed. He isn't much older in feeling than I was fifteen years ago, when I left Vienna — per order Uncle John, as usual. But Uncle John's orders had some sense in them then. Poor Mademoiselle Tavernier! she must be nearly sixty now. I thought my heart was broken ; I was sure of hers. *Sic juvat* — There is something in Virgil which hits it off exactly, — I must brush up my Latin, — something about deep waters and a quiet shore. When Uncle John's letter came I looked upon it as a sentence of transportation for life, and now I am almost as sorry to go home. Home! Which is home, after all? Uncle John is a peremptory old fellow, but he knew what he was about when he sent me away. I know now that I was in a sad, bad way then. The ways of Uncle John are inscrutable. Possibly this present sentence of transportation may turn out for the best. I hope not for life, though. Now I don't think Russell would care if he never saw Hong-Kong again. He growls because I am so deuced rosy about the gills. . . . After all, I am no longer a boy in disgrace. I may properly oppose any mad schemes prompted by Uncle John's affection for his only relatives. I should think the grandniece might have something to say in the matter too.

JUNE 21.—I wonder whether he can have told her of my wild youth? No; of course n⊃t. Still, it would be only right to give her some warning that I have not always been what I now seem. I think the fellows in Hong-Kong all regard me, within rea-sonable business limitations, as a sort of practicable modern saint, just sufficiently mitigated by memories of my own youth to act as father confessor to them. I only hope I am not a prig. Then, Uncle John seemed to think that Nero and Heliogabalus rolled into one were nothing to me. His letter ordering me to go to Hong-Kong was a masterpiece of concise English, and he called me a profligate young scoundrel. True, that time it was by letter : I don't think that even Uncle John would call me a profligate young scoundrel by telegraph. But the dear old fellow had given me a letter of credit for a thousand pounds, and just after I had been dropped from college, too. I certainly ought to have made it last longer than ten months.

And I had been so anxious to go to a German uni-versity ! I had professed such a fondness for books, and begged him so earnestly to send me to Heidel-berg. .And then the way I went off from Heidel-berg—"so dark the manner of my taking off !" I know some one must have written him though about Mademoiselle Tavernier — Ned Wyman, prob-ably — when I wanted to fight that duel about her. Still, it was not quite true to call me a profligate

young scoundrel : it was not my fault that she would
not marry me.   But Uncle John very properly did
not approve of opera singers in the family.   And the
very day I drew my last fifty pounds she disappeared
and left me in Vienna, with no acquaintance but my
creditors, and no friend but the second in the duel I
was to fight.   Only, as it turned out, the other fellow had gone off with her.   I suppose Uncle John
has forgiven me since ; he never referred to it in his
letters. . . . But I hope he has not told Miss Millison.

JUNE 22.—Really, Russell is so happy that he is
almost getting to be a nuisance.   No, I don't quite
mean that ; of course I am glad to see the boy so.   I
suppose I should be just as happy if I were in his
place.   Only he seemed to hold in well enough while
he was in Hong-Kong.   He says he likes to talk to
me about her; I am just old enough.   The weather
is perfect.

JUNE 24.—After all, it seems that Russell is only
eight years younger than I ; hardly that, for he was
born in April and I in December.   When you're both
past thirty, eight years don't make so much difference. . . . Russell is overjoyed to-day because the
ship made 366 miles.   His eagerness to get home is
increasing.   I tell him that is no reason he should
bet every day on the ship's run, though.   As a habit,
it is little better than gambling.

JUNE 27.—Russell showed me a photograph of his
fiancée.   Didn't know he had one ; he didn't show it
to any of the fellows in Hong-Kong.   A pretty girl

enough. . . . I think Uncle John might have sent me out one of his grandniece, by way of sample. Didn't dare, I suppose ; knew I wouldn't come then. She is probably some intellectual creature, whom no one else would fall in love with. I like intelligence in women, but I hate intellect.

JUNE 30.—Had a heavy gale to-day. To-morrow we go into the Red Sea. I had a picture of her mother somewhere ; I must hunt it up. Haven't seen her since the year before I went to college. I've a great mind to tell Russell about the daughter, and ask his advice. He only left the States five years ago, and will know what these girls are like.

JULY 1.—I told Russell of the grandniece to-day. He was really quite enthusiastic. ''Go in, old boy! do go in !'' said he. I told him it was too serious a question to treat flippantly. Then he laughed immoderately at what he called the idea. I don't see what there is so very funny about the idea, nor why he should call me ''old boy'' either. I am only seven years older than he. But you can't be angry with Russell long.

JULY 5.—Saw two big fish and a water-spout. The captain says it is one of the most favorable voyages he ever made. I wish I were sure which way I wanted the ship to go. Russell is getting sentimental.

JULY 6.—Brindisi. Russell has purchased a strip of tickets a yard long, and means to go straight to New York with them. I am not sure they don't even carry him to Mount Desert, where his sweet-heart is. I suppose I must go with him to keep him out of mischief. Profit of foreign travel when you go with a man in love!

July 8.—I am getting weary of this continual railway journeying. And I did want to stop at Rome! Russell got a packet of letters at Brindisi, and takes up all the time reading them. He says there is nothing in them that would interest me. I am not so sure.

July 9.—London. It seems Russell was engaged to Miss Morley before he left Boston. That, of course, is different. Odd, a letter from Uncle John tells me his grandniece is also at Mount Desert, where the Morleys have a cottage. Uncle John writes that she is in love with me already. Great heavens! I wanted to hear a debate in the House of Commons, but Russell will not wait.

July 14.—Mid-Atlantic. Russell becomes more and more sentimental and worse company than ever. Now, I don't consider his state of things a circum-stance to mine. Fancy going to meet a young maid who has, as it were, been instructed to fall in love with you! For I know the cut-and-dried way Uncle John puts things. He told her very much the same way he told me to leave Hong-Kong. I fancy she was more upset than I was, though. Poor girl, how he must have frightened her!

July 19.—New-York. I have had a long talk with Uncle John. It is as I feared. He tells me he has brought up Emily—her name is Emily—with the expectation of marrying me. It is the dearest wish of his declining years, he says. This is a favorite phrase of his, and he repeats it continually. He says it is the dearest wish of her declining years also. I think Russell's example must have worked upon me, for sometimes I catch myself considering as if it were the dearest wish of my declining years. But how the deuce am I to know?—about her dearest wish, I mean. There will, I suppose, be a tell-tale blush when I meet her: in books there is always a tell-tale blush which every one sees but the hero. I must be on the lookout for it. Pshaw! As if I, with my grizzled beard, could cause a tell-tale blush in anybody! Fortunately I am not bald. Russell, I think, is a little bald, and he is quite as gray as I am. Not that we are either of us very gray. He is off to Mount Desert to-morrow. He really seems to enjoy the prospect, and wants me to go with him. So does Uncle John. In other words, he wants the goods delivered as per consignment. I think there ought to be some order from the consignee. It seems she is actually staying with the Morleys.

JULY 20.—Boston. The more I think of it, the more determined I am that I will not go down and gobble up this poor girl perfunctorily, like a Minotaur. Not that I am ill disposed toward her; on the contrary. If I could only get some private way of finding out whether her heart is really as dutiful as Uncle John thinks it is? If I could only be present at our meeting,

and yet not be met,—a dispassionate third party, as
it were,—I think I could tell.   I could then note the
tell-tale blush and other indications.   How curiously
unpractical of Uncle John to think she can really be
in love with a man she has never seen! I might present myself incog., but that trick is used up; besides,
she expects me, and would see through it directly.
Moreover, it would be all up with me the moment
she saw me, I fear.   Uncle John never told her how
old I was, and I never had but one photograph taken,
—in Hong-Kong,—and that was five years ago.

JULY 22.—Rodick's Hotel, Mount Desert.   This is
a curious place.   A great big tinder-box structure
with a huge piazza, several hundred rooms, and almost as many young girls.   The piazza is crowded
with them, and I hardly dare go out there.   When
I do, I catch the eyes of so many of them that I feel I
am blushing myself.   I ought to be beyond blushing, but I am not.   I am afraid I am a very simple
old fellow.   I wonder whether Emily Millison is
among them?   I don't think so.

Russell has been to the Morleys', and come back
disgusted.   He saw nobody.   Miss Morley, not expecting him so soon, is away on a journey to Canada.
This comes of traveling through Europe without
stopping to look at the scenery.   Uncle John's niece
is there, and I am to go and see her to-morrow.

EVENING.—She was pointed out to me to-night
driving by the hotel.   She seems to be a pretty girl.
Poor thing, how she must dread my arrival! It was

absurd in me to fall in with Uncle John's preconceived notion so easily in New-York. A young girl like her, really attractive, too, with probably half the young fellows in town at her feet. But in this instance common humanity dictates that Uncle John should be thwarted. I won't trouble her long.

JULY 23.—I have just had a brilliant idea. It came to me in my dream, Why shouldn't Russell be presented in my place? He is complaining of nothing to do. Then I can go with him—as Mr. Russell—and watch how they behave. If she loves him she will, metaphorically speaking, rush into his arms. If she does that, I will disclose myself at once. . . . I have just spoken to Russell. He seems rather pleased at the idea. But he laughs at what he terms my quixotic scruples, and says if she doesn't care for me she will say so. I have a feeling she will be too modest, too shy, too submissive. Russell doesn't know Uncle John. He says I don't know American girls. I have always noticed a certain want of ideal in Russell. He agrees with me, however, in thinking that Uncle John was probably mistaken in the warmth of her affections toward me. Still, it is quite understood between us that if she does rush into his arms, he is to hand her over to me at once. We have timed our call at dusk, so there can be no prejudice of age or faces. . . . This afternoon we went to drive. I never saw so many young people all out-doors together at once. I wondered whether Miss Millison could be among them ; but every maiden

had a youth by her side, and I could not but hope
the contrary.   Even a youth would be no despicable
rival for an old fellow like me.

6 P. M.—She just passed through the hall of the
hotel.   I hope she will give me—that is, Russell—a
warm reception to-night.   Ought she to kiss him?
No ; that would be too much.   The pressure of the
hand, the glance of the eye shyly looking up, will
tell it all.   Odd, I don't think that a month ago I
should have minded her kissing him — except on
her account. . . . I have just been to tea, and
Russell is dressing.   I do hope he will put on a be-
coming coat.   First impressions amount to something even in a future husband selected by Uncle
John.   I tried to drop Russell a hint just now, but
he didn't seem to understand. . . . The sun is
setting, and the village street is full of girls.   It is a
lovely sight.   Beyond lies the bay with moonlight
accompaniment ; I am growing sentimental.   At
my age it is almost improper. . . . I have just
been to hurry up Russell.   He got quite angry with
me because I criticised his coat.   I am sure I should
wear a black coat if I were going to call on my
fiancée for the first time.   I have been giving him a
few points on Uncle John, that he may carry off the
situation.   And if Uncle John's vagary should haply
prove well founded, we are to pretend that it was all
a mistake taking him for me.   Here goes for the tell-
tale blush !

10 P.M.—It is all over.   I don't see how I could
have been such a fool; I was sensible enough when

I left Hong-Kong. We called at eight, sent up our cards ; that is, I sent up Russell's and he sent up mine. Emily—Miss Millison—was out on the piazza with a lanky youth called Tim Chipman, who removed himself awkwardly from the field. While Russell went forward, I lurked behind one of the pillars, with the light well behind me, to mark the tell-tale blush. But instead of blushing she turned a little pale, I thought, and could not speak for several seconds ; just as if it were a terrible moment which she had hoped would never arrive. Finally, " How do you do, Mr. Witherspoon?" said she, almost with a tone of sarcasm (my name does have a ludicrous sound if you dwell upon it too much), and hardly left her hand in his a second. And I will swear that at that moment Russell had the heart to look around at me and grin. The meeting was over so much sooner than I expected that I had no time to get out from behind the pillar, but stumbled about among the chairs in the dark while Russell was introducing me as his friend, Mr. Russell, and I could see that she was a little angry with me, even, because I was the friend of her unwelcome husband that was to be. It was easy to see how she hated him, though it was quite dark ; for she hardly looked toward him once again, but spoke pointedly all the evening to me. I think Russell was much piqued that he had made so ineffectual an impression, but what was his pique to my disappointment—being an eye-witness of the horror with which she regarded the match ! So I told Russell, and he got quite angry with me, and called her a silly little chit. I wish she were ! But she is a sweet, intelligent woman ; I must do Uncle John the justice to admit it. Heigho ! here ends my day-dream. I am off to-morrow.

JULY 24.—Russell begs me to stay a few days with him ; at least, until his lady-love gets back. It is a lovely morning, and I am half inclined to do so. He insists that I overrated Miss Millison's coldness to him last night, and that she squeezed his hand on parting. It is only wounded *amour propre* that makes him say this. But he insists also on going to see her this morning, and meantime I am going out for a sail. I have just had a telegram from Uncle John, saying he was coming down to bring his formal congratulations. Replied, "For God's sake, don't do anything of the kind"; but the telegraph girl seemed to think this was too strong, so had to send, "Please don't be such a fool," which was ruder, if less profane. But nothing weaker would have stopped Uncle John.

I P.M.—Russell has just returned, and declares that she received him perfectly. According to his account, she talked as if the idea of marrying a middle-aged Hong-Kong merchant had grown with her so from early infancy as to be part of her very being. One would think that I, John Witherspoon, aged eight-and-thirty, were the Prince Charming of her fairy tales ; that is, the idea of me, temporarily incarnated in Russell. Russell swears that he kissed her hand, which I do not believe. He would have the audacity to say that she kissed him if he thought

I would swallow it. Still, he has almost persuaded me to try it a few days longer. He says he is willing to keep up the travesty if I am. I shall try to win her esteem as the old friend of her lover.

JULY 26.—I am afraid the old friend plan does not work very well. The moment I get at all fatherly in my manner she seems frightened, and looks to Russell as if for protection. And she has been very cold to me since, as if there were something dishonest or ungentlemanly in my advances. And when I called this afternoon there was a youth calling there too, and she wouldn't let him go while I was there. His name was Chipman—Tim Chipman. Can there be anything between them, I wonder? Or is she really offended with my friendly advances? I suppose I ought to remember that she thinks I am Russell, and engaged to Miss Morley, her friend. Can it be that she really takes me for thirty-one? I am fairly not old-looking for my age; and she is twenty-one. Russell still thinks that I am a great fool, and that her heart is in the match with me; that is, as she thinks, with him. Russell is an ass.

JULY 27.—I wish I could persuade myself that Russell is right, and that it is not all the conceit of an advocate. I have a great mind to make love to her in earnest as Russell. If she really cares for her uncle's wishes, she will repel me with more scorn than ever. Then all will be well. But if, in her desire to escape from such cut-and-dried matrimony, she grasps at the first straw that presents itself,—even

at me,—I shall know that Uncle John was, as I suspected at Hong-Kong, little better than a fool at love
affairs, though a good enough business man in other
respects.

EVENING.—I have dressed myself as young as possible, and am going there alone. Tim Chipman is a
nuisance ; he was there all the afternoon. Boys of
that age haven't any business to be loafing down
here with young women at the sea-shore ; they ought
to have some steady occupation. When I was Tim
Chipman's age I was sent to Hong-Kong.

NIGHT.—True to my regular habits, I must write
in my journal as usual, though the events of the
evening verge on tragedy. I went there, and was
admitted. I furnished some weak excuse for Witherspoon's absence—she did not seem deeply grieved.
This was already a bad sign, I thought, as I sat down
a little nearer to her than usual. She seemed sad,
and if I read her eyes aright by the soft glow of the
lamp, there was a tender dimness in them as of tears
she had not yet forgotten. Ah, mine uncle, my kind
old uncle, you should not have called your middle-
aged nephew back home again only to break his
middle aged heart !

Well, well ! how it began I do not know. There
was some talk of Hong-Kong and Mount Desert, and
of Uncle John, and of artificial marriages, and of love
and misery, and of her and me, and I thought she
was going to cry, and I took her hand, and, by
Heaven, I kissed it. Oh, the artful, miserable girl !

the light, unfaithful, contemptible coquette! She let me kiss her. She, as she supposes, engaged to another man, and he a most worthy fellow, and nephew to her uncle who has been more than a father to her; and I, engaged to another woman, and that woman her dearest friend and hostess, now temporarily absent, and she breaks her plighted troth, and the most sacred obligations of friendship, and the dearest wish of her elderly uncle's declining years, at my first smile, at the very first advance of the first middle-aged stranger who makes bold to kiss her! Ah, American girls, the half has not been told! Daisy Miller, you are a mere mitigation of the naked truth!

I suppose the horror of my expression after that fatal salute must have been apparent to her, for she started back in alarm. It is, of course, unusual for a man who has been shown the signal favor of a kiss to appear shocked or enraged. But I could not conceal from her all that I felt. At the instant I had seen the kiss about to become a realization, all my heart for mockery had left me, and I had dropped her hand as carelessly as if it were a burned-out match.

Probably most men look pleased when a pretty girl allows them to kiss her, and my bearing must have seemed eccentric. She drew back and blushed. She did have the grace to blush. And I was silent. At one moment I was on the point of kissing her again; then, of leaving her forever. It was the latter course that I finally adopted. She, I presume, was awaiting a more explicit avowal — waiting for me to show my treason to my friend, as she had proved her treason to her troth.   Uncle John, you built your hopes on shifting sand.

JULY 28.—Now am I fit for stratagem and spoil. So far, I have always been ingenuous and sincere ; but the duplicity of this woman would disarm the compassion of a pelican. I won't go away. Why should I? I have no place else to go to — except back to Hong-Kong.   Some time, I hope, I may go home to Hong-Kong, but not now.   Here will I stay and see this tragedy to its end.   Russell's young woman is to arrive to-morrow ; but I have begged him to take her into the secret for a day at least, that I may see how far this woman's perversity may go.   I am convinced that if it had not been that Russell was presented to her in the trying light of duty, and I in that of idle and perverse amusement, she never would have preferred me to him.   As it is, even with an elderly guide like myself, the wayward path is the flowery one to her.

JULY 29.—Russell's girl has returned.   She seems a nice, true creature.   Pity she is not so attractive as Emily Millison.   Little she knows what a faithless friend she has in her.   We have great difficulty in getting her to consent to our plot, even for a day or two, as, of course, it separates her from Russell, and gives her to me instead.   It is remarkable how much she cares for him — a careless fellow, who doesn't deserve it.

Can Miss Millison be only flirting? Not that that would be any excuse for her; but though I have left her for Miss Morley, she seems to bear it calmly enough. It ought to surprise her, after our scene of the other night.

JULY 30.—Russell is beginning to growl at being kept so long from his sweetheart. Some men have no discrimination. Now, if he knew what a nuisance it is to be always at Miss Morley's beck and call. I suppose she may be attractive to some men, but she is wholly lacking in intelligence.

3 P. M.—We have been to walk. I have a more terrible suspicion still. Can it be that she is not only doubly but trebly false? We walked in the woods, and sat down in a damp, mossy sort of place at the foot of an oak-tree—I, of course, with Miss Morley, Russell with Emily Millison. I took advantage of Miss Morley's going to sleep to walk around the tree and see what they were doing. Russell got up and left, and she and I entered into conversation. With fine irony I deplored her fate in being married off by her uncle. With irony, I say, for the line of conduct she sees fit to pursue in the premises makes any commiseration superfluous. But she chimed in, as if she were the enchanted princess in a fairy tale, and Uncle John the ogre. She hinted that my caress the other day was prompted by fatherly pity alone (I'll be hanged if it was!), and that it was the rarity of kind treatment which moved her to tears. Then she went on to speak of old suitors and young lovers, as if Tim

Chipman were the man, after all. Kind treatment, indeed! If she expects every man to coax away her moods with a kiss, I hope it is a rarity. But I fancy it won't be long. I must warn Uncle John against Chipman. A boy with no visible occupation at twenty-three will surely take to vicious courses sooner or later. Why, I myself— But then I was younger at the time of the Tavernier episode. When I went back to the other side of the tree, I found the Morley girl awake again, and Russell with her. They were parted with some difficulty, and have flatly refused to go on for another day.

I shall bring on the catastrophe to-night. Possibly Mr. Tim Chipman could do it better, but I will try. I must see how far that girl will go.

MIDNIGHT.—I have found out. We have been to row in a boat, Emily Millison and I. I went around and asked her, after tea, and she accepted readily, though, as she could not have known that Russell did not mean to call, I had hardly expected it. We started about sunset; the sea was silent, and soon the moon came out, large and round, above the peak of Green Mountain. We rowed across the bay alone, and landed on Bald Porcupine, a solitary rocky islet covered with small firs. I was sorry that she consented to land, but it gave me the brutal nerve I needed. It was my part to play the impassioned lover, and I did so recklessly and relentlessly. Even then and there she did not shrink. It became horribly evident that she was luring me on.

It was terrible. I began to pity even Chipman. I could feel the cold sweat on my forehead. I forgot that she was Uncle John's niece. My irritation — to use no stronger term — forced me beyond all bounds. Clasping her hand (the night was warm and light, the waves scarcely murmuring on the rocks, moonlight, and all that sort of thing ; just such a night as when Jessica's, or Lady Julia's, or all other love affairs or elopements have been carried out) — clasping her hand, again I kissed it ; and she seeming nothing loath, but rather leaning toward me still more, I swore to her that I loved no one but her. I told her that I cared nothing for Miss Morley ; that I had been engaged to her in my early youth ; but that since I had seen her, Emily (I called her Emily), the other had been naught to me. I told her that her betrothal out of hand to a man she had never seen could not be binding ; that her Uncle John was a tyrant — I lied even to that extent ; and I said that I (Russell) knew myself (Witherspoon) to be a profligate. Even that cowardly, backbiting slander on the man she supposed herself engaged to did not rouse her indignation. Finally, I clasped her in my arms and besought her to leave him and fly with me. And, by Heavens, she said she would !

Then, indeed, I rose, and with a bitter laugh denounced her. I dropped her hand upon the bank, and told her that I scorned her treasonable love. And she laughed ! She seemed without a vestige of a conscience, and my invective became so strong that at last I was grimly pleased to see her cry. Finally, she cried so much that I was forced to soothe her a little. I feared she might become hysterical. She had something clasped in her hand, and was weeping over it strangely and unnaturally. I looked at it: it was a photograph. The photograph of a fourth? I took it from her and held it up to the moonlight. It was mine. It was one I had taken in Hong-Kong five years ago. Uncle John had sent it to her before my arrival.

Emily was still crying, but laughing a little too.

"How long have you known me?" I asked her.

"From the first, of course," she said, "when your friend Mr. Russell was presented as yourself— as Mr. Witherspoon." And the little drawl she gave my name recalled to me at once her sarcastic, offended manner of receiving me.

When we got to talking about practical things — that is, just now — I began to blame her a little for her deceit. She asked me what I thought of mine. I had no answer ready at the moment. So I told her we ought to write to Uncle John at once. The old fellow will be so much pleased !

JULY 31.—I am not going back to Hong-Kong. We are to live in New-York. Tim Chipman is going to Hong-Kong.

I must reserve the last page of my journal for some commissions I have to do for Emily in the city. So this is the

END OF VOL. XIV.

October.

In a Garret.

TO BE READ THERE, IN AN AUTUMN STORM.

T happened only last September; and I think you do not know her. I should not, but for my old aunt Abby; but now I often look at her when I meet her in the street, in her faded black gown,—is it bombazine, or is it alpaca?—that is so limp and dingy and worn-out and looks like mourning tired with too many years' wearing. Happily her face belies its frame: she has a sweet face, still pretty, and very fresh and smooth and quiet. Aunt Abby says she is far from poor; she knows her as working in some old charities, to which she gives much money. I asked about her when I heard it, and found out more than Aunt Abby knows. Indeed, these things are not usually known; and I think I found out more than any one knows, although this is a true story.

You see, Garden street is not a pleasant street, and
very few people know of it, and still fewer would
ever go there; and to visit in Garden street is more
than one would do for a mere acquaintance. It was
not out of any want of respect for Miss Allerton, but
she was so very old that her friends were mostly
infirm, or dead, or they had many descendants and
engrossing family cares; and she had no relatives, or,
at least, none in Boston — at all events, none near
enough to expect to come in for any of her money;
and mere acquaintances, as I have said, could not be
expected to go to Garden street to see her. Then,
Miss Allerton had no nephews or great-nephews to
keep her name before people, and no pretty-faced
nieces to bring her on the scene as aunt to Juliet and
a person for Romeos to conciliate. Then, she lived
on Garden street — in a court off Garden street.
Now, Garden street is bad enough, but Garden Court
is worse; for court is not a courtly name, like square
or avenue. I, for one, if I die rich, expect to end my
days on a boulevard at least, as names go now in the
Republic.

Thus even the mere geography of the thing was
enough; for few people having due self-respect and
sense of their position, social and geographical, in
Backbavia, would care to be found north of Cambridge
street; and there were still fewer people left in
society of social creation sufficiently remote to remember that they should continue to know Miss
Allerton simply because she was Miss Allerton and

her father had been Judge Allerton, who was the son of Harry Allerton, Governor of the King's Province of Massachusetts Bay. But charity covers a multitude of sins; a lady with a subscription-paper for soup can venture even to the end of Hanover street, in a coupé; and that is why Miss Allerton's calls had come to be mostly associated with subscription-papers. Lady and gentlemen almoners knew that Miss Allerton was sure for twenty dollars or so, which she always paid in a roll of clean bank-bills, never by a check. Indeed, it was hard to imagine her respectable name at the foot of a national bank-check; doubtless it would have been dishonored. In fact, Miss Allerton was a very musty and obsolete old person indeed — though she still went on, like an old eight-day clock that has never been subjected to modern repairs.

The first time I went down there (*I* went with a subscription-paper) the venerable lady did not come to the door, and I asked the maid-servant if she were in. The servant herself, as a door-tender, showed signs of desuetude: she made one or two throaty noises, such as a mechanical toy would make if it attempted to execute a new squeak, and said that Miss Allerton was engaged. This reply seemed as difficult to her as a repartee to an echo, and the moment she had made it her skin turned browner with the blush that mantled over the enormity of the lie she had told.

For Miss Allerton at that moment was sitting in her attic, doing nothing, and it was a falsehood most preposterous to say that she was not at home.

As I have said, the house was on a court; but at
least it had the court to itself.   Garden street leaves
Hutchinson street and runs down toward the water
behind the jail, through what used to be the Mill-
pond, a district now filled in with the scum of
humanity.   After you leave Cambridge street you go
between a line of houses, ordinary enough two-and-
a-half-story bricks, with the door-way in an arched
cell, and often a pasteboard placard in the window,
"Rooms to Let, with Board."   The basements are
usually filled with shoemakers or grocers, and here
and there an undertaker with a red ticket in the window, "Ice."   By and by you see that the houses are
older, by the "bind" of the bricks, laying the ends and
sides of the bricks alternating, and not in our monotonous modern way.   The basement windows make
a display of round bundles of kindling-wood and
square cakes of popped corn cemented with treacle.
Even these houses have seen better days.   Occasionally you may note a large arched front door with a
fan-light of glass over it, or the frieze of a house
moulded in little wooden squares;   there is an old
wooden sign of a Saracen or other painted heathen
perched on a bracket above a door where a negro
politician keeps a pool-room.   And just before you
get to a corner where there is a gin-shop and a fashionable dress-maker, you turn up to the left into
Garden Court, of which the wall on one side is made
by a mossy wooden building skirting a discolored bit
of grass, where there is an elm and a skinned and

moribund sycamore. Miss Allerton's house faces upon this bit of grass, presenting to it a yellow façade with two gables, and only an edge to the street. The house would seem to have turned a cold shoulder to the street since it took to evil company. In the southernmost of the two gables is the garret in which Miss Allerton sat. There is a bedroom in the end toward the street; the gable does not run clear through the house, but stops and sinks down into a sloping roof with a dormer window in it. This is the garret window: it looks toward the river; and you can still see a rood or so of green water between the piles of the drawbridge and the Fitchburg Railway-Station.

When the servant had shut the door in my face, I went back and told my uncle (who had sent me down with the subscription-paper) that Miss Allerton was engaged. He could not have been more surprised if I had said she was engaged to be married. He wondered who took care of the old lady now; and I asked if she lived up in that neighborhood all alone; and he said that he didn't know, but supposed she was rich enough to have some poor relation with her. I did not ask him then who she was, because I knew that Aunt Abby would be more likely to know; and, indeed, I was desirous of getting uptown, for I wished to get my ride that evening, and also had to go to a dinner-party.

I rode home along the quay, just before sunset; but there was no knowing the exact time, for the

autumn mist was on the river, which might have
been a sea for any sign that was visible of an opposite coast. A rod from the shore the smooth olive
water faded to gray, and soon vanished, with no
horizon-line, only the hull of a distant ship shadowed
in. It was depressing; but the prospect of dinner
and bright dresses was before me, and I rode the
faster as the mist began to ravel out and a cold dash
of rain came from the east. I even enjoyed the
scene,—it was such a delicious contrast to an evening of gayety,—and I stopped a moment, when
nearly home, to look again at the river, now ruffled
by the wind that brought the rain. The same dash
of rain pattered down on the roof of Miss Allerton's
garret, and she sighed and turned her eyes back from
the window to the littered floor and the dusty boxes.
She had been doing nothing all the afternoon, and it
was now nearly five.

It was almost as unusual for Miss Allerton to be
idle as it was for her to be depressed: she had lived
before boredom was discovered, and was too unfashionable to have learned it since. And, although
Miss Allerton was somewhat sad at heart, sitting to-
day in the garret, she was not at all a querulous old
lady. So far was she from being unhappy that she
had sat there and forgotten to leave the place, more
in wonder at her mood than because of it. She was
used to taking this world cheerfully, as having a
heaven-sent meaning in it. She had not felt sorrow
for so many years: perhaps that was the reason of it.

It had been rainy for a week, and her old servant had
talked of leaving her, and one of her poor families
had been found without sobriety. Not that there was
very much in all this, but it troubled her a little; and
then she had gone up into the garret at one, just
after dinner, and had opened an old trunk to get
some old dress to give away, and the idle fit had
come on her, and she had stayed there ever since.

A pleasant face had Miss Allerton — a very pleasant face, with the soft gray hair and the kind
wrinkles near the eyes. There was a spinning-
wheel near her, and a row of old painted chests ;
fire-irons, a pompous old cane, silk-worked samplers,
a rubber fire-bucket, an old wig, and doubtless many
other family relics were stowed away in the boxes
about her. The lozenge-shaped frame of some old
dowager Allerton's hatchment was leaning with its
face to the wall, falling to pieces, slowly, with the
inseparable air of leisure and dignity that attaches to
things which have outlived their use. Miss Allerton,
too, had been thinking that she had outlived her use,
and she looked vacantly at an old leather bag hanging
on a nail in the wall, evidently empty. The leather
bag had hung there many a year, but she had never
noticed it before. Then she looked out of the little
dormer window, and over to the wharves, and the
factories, and the rows of wooden houses, and the
dirty river slipping through its grove of piles, and all
the horizon of huddled houses where she remembered
green meadows and wooded hills and a blue river,

when her eyes were blue, not gray, nor meant for use alone.

She paused to assure herself that she was not unhappy. Surely not,—even in the garret there, looking out on the damp, dull weather; a little lonely, that was all. And she had had so many friends! Then she remembered — what woman ever forgets? — a fair girl she had known, about the time Lafayette came to town, who was very pretty, sweetly, dearly pretty. It was odd to think this girl had been herself. There was no vanity in remembering this, for it did not seem to be herself,— rather some daughter of hers who had long been dead. Only, she had never had any children. Then, her father, the judge,— the proud old gentleman whom all the little provincial city had known and liked to honor,— there were so few people left in the town now, although it had grown so large. Somewhat too proud indeed was he, she thought, with a sigh, in the days when the crowded wooden house was a mansion with a garden that stretched back to the square old stone houses of their friends in Bowdoin Square. After all, the time might come when she would have to leave the old house, old and unfashionable as it was, for the family fortune had grown out of fashion too, and the square brick warehouses were out of date and yielded little rent now; and she had never had the heart to cut down her list of charities. She had thought the fortune would outlast her time; but she had lived too long. Not that she cared much for the fortune, but her friends had often told her she must move: the street was no longer respectable. After all, though, it was not so very lonely there. She liked it better than another place. But it was a dreary September day; it was the equinoctial,—there was no doubt of that; just such a day as it had been in that September in 1832 when her father, the stern old judge, had come and told her.

Yet it was strange; it still seemed as strange as it did on that first day. It had never been explained. He surely had loved her; she had thought so on that very first day of all, when the young stranger was introduced to her at her father's friend's, at a tea-party. How near, too, she had been to giving up the tea-party that night! She had a headache from the ball the night before, and she was a proud young beauty, and there was going to be no one there but a new clerk of Mr. Oliver's, some young man who had come North from the Carolinas, or from some sugar-plantation in Barbadoes. He certainly was attracted by her that night; and he asked permission to attend her home, and her father refused it. Yes, her father had been born among the colonial aristocracy, and he was very proud.

But she had tried to make it all up, so far as she modestly could; he was not used to her father's ways, but he was a frank, ingenuous young gentle-man, who had won his way with every one. Only he had been very shy, and very much afraid of her, and very modest. It had been a twelvemonth

before she had blushed when they met, so gentle had
he been in his wooing, and then a year again before
he dared to take her hand and look at her and leave
her as he did that night of the election.   And then,
of course, she had supposed that he would come to
see her father the next day ; and every one spoke well
of him by that time,— every one, even her father,
the old judge.   But he had never come.   And the
next day (or was it a week after ?) her father — it was
just such a day as this, with the mist, and the damp,
and the wind blowing the fog — her father had come
home to tea, and had told her (he had said so casu-
ally, she remembered, in the hall, as she had been
helping to divest him of his surtout) — had told her
that young F—— was gone to the Californias.   And
that same old mail-bag had been hanging in the hall.

She had been angry at first, but she had long since
given over being angry ; and it was not long after
that when the old judge died and left her with one
brother.   He had not done very well in the world ;
and he had died too.   And many years after she saw
in the newspaper that Mr. F—— had died in the Californias.   (She had never mentioned the name to any
one in fifty years, nor shall I do so.)   She had seen
F—— once after the time he had looked in her eyes
on that election-day,— but only in the street, and
she was in her carriage, and she was a little piqued
and had feigned not to see him ; and it was the day
after this that her father had come home and told her,
in the hall.   She was wondering even then why he

had not come; it was already the beginning of that long wonder that was to make a puzzle of her life,—until, indeed, she grew middle-aged, and had found her work to do; and since then she had been very happy. Only she wished that she might have had young relations; her brother had left no children. For many years she still had thought that he would write; but he never did. Could it be that he had '. never loved at all? It was very strange.

Here again she paused a moment in her thinking and looked again across the river. It had not always been fretted with so many bridges. They used to have to drive many miles around to the old house at Lechmere's Point, just across the stream. She wondered if the house was still there; now there were many high blocks about it, where the orchards had been, and a dozen long black bridges stretched out and away, like the arms of the great city reaching for the woods and fields. She got up and walked to the window, with a rustle of her clean silk gown, and looked out for the view of country highlands. But the mist and fog were too thick. You never would have thought her seventy-odd as she stood there with her pleasant face and her bright eyes peering as a girl's might do for some arrival. Then she looked back into the garret with the mass of old things stored away,— the outworn symbols of her quiet life. There was a lack of children's toys and little chairs; most of the things were very old, from the locks in the chests to the old leather mail-bag on the wall. It

was all hers,— hers alone. Half a thousand children
passed by her windows every day, noisy, unkempt
children, to a school near by, and they would look up
to her windows and cry out at her. People thought
she was a miser and hoarded more than memories.
And the neighborhood was very sad and squalid, and
people said it was not even safe for her to live there.
· She was very old. Had he died happily? she thought.
The paper said that he had never been married. And
yet he had behaved so cruelly to her. He had pleasant brown eyes, and such a brave, manly way about
him ! And then how tenderly he had taken the posy
from her ! Why was it that she thought of him to-
day? And she remembered thinking, years before,
that she would never have to cry again.

She felt that she was doing wrong, and tried to
scold herself like a child. Wiping her old eyes with
a girl's light touch to the eyes and head, she got up
and went to the window again resolutely. The fog
and rain were still driving from the sea. Almost in
the zenith was a little break of pale-blue sky, so pure,
so cold, that it seemed like a memory of heaven ; and
its color showed that it was after sunset. She heard
a crash behind her ; it was a startling sound in the
still garret, but she turned and saw that it was only
the old mail-bag fallen to the floor. It had hung upon
its hook half a century, and at last the ribbon had
broken with the weight.

Miss Allerton remembered it well,—how it had
hung upon the knob of her father's door and been

carried by him to his office and back on days when foreign ships came in. It was very dusty, but she stooped to pick it up, and her hand slipped in through the leathern lips and drew forth a letter. It was a letter that had never been opened. It must have stuck in a wrinkle in the bottom of the bag and lain there all these years. It was too dark in the old garret to see more than that it was folded over and sealed with a great, careless seal, without a stamp. It was evidently written before the days of stamps. She walked with it to the little window: the little square of blue sky had grown larger, and gave just light enough for her old eyes to read the address,— to her,—to Madam Sarah Allerton.

It was a boyish, trembling handwriting, but the sight of it set her heart beating as it might have done a girl's. She steadied herself on the window-sill a minute before she broke the seal. The letter ran as follows :

Sept. the 8th, 1832.

"DEAR MADAM,—If I dare to write to you to ask your leave to lay my addresses before your respected father, it is only that I feel last night that you learned my secret. I am too unworthy of you not to deem this letter presumptuous: forgive me, dear Miss Allerton, if you cannot return my love. If you smile when next we meet, I will take it that you are not angry with me, although you cannot deign to love me. For I have loved you since that day we met two years ago. But if you can neither love nor pardon me, make no answer to this note, and I shall know.

" F——.

" Dearest, I do love you so ! "

Miss Allerton dropped the letter from her hands and looked outward at the sky.   The rain was driving now, washing the heavens clear; and the rain came also from her eyes, and tears unwonted fell upon the dusty garret floor.   But he had loved her: that was all.   A last time she looked over the old river: the clear rift of blue was wider now, and the curtain of rain swept back across the bay, from where the long gray cloud-bank rose away from the clear horizon.   The autumn storm was over, and under its clear blue rim there came the winter.

But I think of late Miss Allerton has been happier and less lonely than of old.   And I do assure you she is a very dear old lady, young-looking for her years.

November.

A Tale Unfolded.

A STORY FOR MIDNIGHT, AFTER THE FIRST DINNER
PARTY OF THE SEASON.

AM not one of those who cannot let well enough alone. My main object in this world is comfort. And I always thought it a most signal nuisance, after things had got so quietly and nicely fixed at Elsinore, that all those old matters of times past should have been gone into and stirred up as they were by Hamlet. It is true, on the one hand, you had a king—good. He had been a good king in his day, I do not gainsay it, but dead and buried now. On the other hand, you had a queen who (whatever amiable weaknesses she may have been guilty of in times gone by) was then living in undeniable holy matrimony with his majesty the king regnant—good. The *convenances* were all properly observed. I never heard that any particular European scandal attached at the time to the court of Denmark. To be sure, there was Ophelia—but that, again, was Hamlet's fault; I am coming to him. He was the discordant element. Meantime, the season at Elsinore bade fair to be particularly gay—for the reigning king was most popular in society—and everything might have gone on comfortably. Good.

"Then in comes this fellow Hamlet (who, be it said, might have been infinitely better employed fighting Fortinbras than in chancing pot-shots behind arrases), a robustious prating man-about-town, for all his assumed culture and university airs, who conducts himself in a manner wholly devoid of tact and *savoir-faire!* And, of course, he spoiled everything. Don't you think so, Mrs. de Monégo?"

Mrs. de Monégo cast up her beautiful eyes at mine, and then as languidly let them fall upon a turquoise brooch upon her neck. And I followed them with mine, as Mrs. de Monégo intended that I should. "You're such a wag, Mr. Wraye," said she; "how do you keep it up?"

"You've such a beautiful neck and shoulders," thought I; "how do you keep them from getting sunburned?" But, of course, I did not say it, but went on looking at the turquoise brooch, and just then the first grave-digger threw out a skull with a thud upon the stage. The skull was a real one—I should say it might have been living in the seventeenth century—and it looked up brownly at us and grinned.

It had been a most gay season in Philadelphia; the Philadelphians all spoke of it with suppressed enthusiasm, as of a religious revival. Dinners had followed lunches and five-o'clock teas; balls had succeeded dinners and ended in suppers; and suppers were hardly over before the *déjeûners dansants* of the next day began. And we were both happy. Mrs. de Monégo thought she had made sure of the fourteenth bouquet for the morrow's assembly; I was looking forward to a terrapin supper to which we were all bidden to meet the Hamlet and Ophelia of the play. But that supper proved to be a very mysterious and terrible occasion, both to Mrs. de Monégo and to me.

The Hamlet and Ophelia were from London, and starring it in America; our jolly party, Mrs. de Monégo, Van Knyper, myself, and other young New-Yorkers, had run over to Philadelphia to star it a week in the provinces; and young Hay Diddle was to give us all terrapin and old Madeira at twelve. We were to do the eating, and Hamlet and Ophelia—that is, Norval and Miss Tree—were expected to do the entertaining. What form the entertainment would assume we did not then foresee; or Diddle would not have bidden us, and we should surely not have accepted. No one not of this world can be *du grand monde;* ours is an exclusive set, and we draw the line at ghosts.

Philadelphia has always seemed to me a sort of Mahomet's paradise—a city after Omar Khayyam's own heart. Here are bulbuls and bonbons, ghazuls and demoiselles, wine, roses, and terrapin. Philadelphians never reflect. It is all they can do to digest. But I am nervous New-Yorker, and too much food is food for too much reflection. The pall came over me about the beginning of the fifth act; the general *battue* of the

chief persons of the drama which Hamlet indulges in
at the end failed to cheer me up; and as we drove to
Diddle's apartments I began to reflect violently, and
about the most unpleasant things—not of the carriages, white satin cloaks and perfumes, but of stables,
shrouds, and drains; not of brilliant gas lights and
flowers, but of coal tar and mould; not of cut glass
and laces, but of penury and toil. This gay life was
merely sensuous, earthly, material. Well, these
other things were material and sensuous, too. It
was all of a piece; could we always keep off the
seamy side? The right side of the soil is only just
tolerable, with frequent baths; how about the wrong
side, where, after all, the greatest part of eternity
we mortals are bound to spend? Thus thinking, I
appeared dull to my companion, and she snubbed me.

" You are *distrait*," said she.

"Madam," said I, "one place is as real as another. The exterior of your boudoir is lovely, but
how about the rats and rubble in the plaster?"

" You are coarse," Mrs. de Monégo replied; and
she would none of me, but addressed the rest of her
charming glances to Van Knyper.

Hay Diddle had most delightful apartments. They
were crammed with objects of great rarity,—old
weapons, jewels, musical instruments,—all connected with some history of crime or some pleasant
court story of the easy days of old: swords of
bigotry, and jeweled objects valuable as virtue in
exchange; and, with other objects of *bijouterie* and

vertu, in the place of honor of the oldest and most curious cabinet of all, a human skull reposed, just such another as we had seen upon the stage. But at first we did not see this ; none of the ladies had eyes for a sku'l, and we all looked at the ladies' eyes. Norval, the keen tragedian, saw it first. It was after we had all had coffee, and the conversation turned on ghosts. Why, I cannot imagine. It would have been very hard on a fellow to be a ghost just then, with all the good things upon the table and all the pretty things around it. It would have been a sad lot for any ghost who may have lurked behind the Japanese screen and looked at pretty Daisy Rittenhouse and Posie McGlitter and Mrs. de Monégo. He must have wished himself back in the flesh again, with blood in his cheeks, a spotless white shirt over his cold ribs, and evening dress instead of a shroud !

"Speaking of ghosts," said Norval,— and we all gave a little preparatory shudder of attention, for we felt that the great tragedian was about to begin to amuse us,— "I have known some very queer things connected with skulls. Where did you get that one of yours, Mr. Diddle? A fine specimen."

Diddle said that some actor had given it to him.

"I should like to see it," said Norval. "I have known some skulls that could talk."

"Oh, delightful, Mr. Norval!" cried Mrs. de Monégo. "What a fascinating idea ! It quite makes the cold shivers run down my back ! Do let us try this one !" I thought Miss McGlitter seemed a trifle less charmed ; Van Knyper looked at Mrs. de Monégo's back ; and I am sure pretty Daisy Rittenhouse thought her coarse. But coarseness is the mode, just now. A servant brought the skull to Norval, and he examined it gravely.

" See the bulge over the eyes," Mrs. de Monégo, said he ; " observe the breadth of the occiput ! What strength of purpose this fellow must have had, conjoined with what ideality ! What soul he must have poured into those long-vanished eyes of his — when he talked to some fair lady ! And feel how hard and smooth the cranium ! "

Thus urged, Mrs. de Monégo daintily touched the brown bone with her soft finger : just touched, and no more ; and then shrank back, with a little scream.

" It feels, Mr. Norval — it feels, I am sure. Oh, I know it can talk ! Do try, if you know the way to make it speak ? "

All the rest of us were silent. " I have once heard of such a thing," said the actor. " I might try, if you like. But remember, I am not responsible for what it says."

Mrs. de Monégo laughed joyously. " It can say nothing to offend us. I think we have the advantage of position, don't you ? We are better dressed ! "

No one else spoke ; but no one made objection. I don't think our host half liked it. However, a Dresden china platter was brought ; and the skull was placed in it upon the table. Norval gave directions for the lights to be turned down, and the servants to be removed. Then he regarded the skull intently for some minutes. The room was most intensely silent. Van Knyper lighted a cigarette. The darkness was such that I could just see the glimmer of diamonds and the round, white shoulders of Mrs. de Monégo, sitting opposite. Whether shivers were already running down her back, it was impossible to say. We were silent several minutes. Then a voice came; but for the life of me, I could not tell whether it was the skull or Norval speaking—

> " I could a tale unfold whose lightest word
> Would harrow up thy soul, freeze thy young blood,
> Make thy two eyes, like stars, start from their spheres,
> Thy knotted and combined locks to part,
> Like quills upon the fretful porcupine."

We were breathless. It seemed to me, as I looked upon the skull, that there was a faint, unwholesome shine in the sockets of what had been its eyes. And I will swear that from the dry bone, clean and polished as it was, there came an earthly, mortal smell as of the grave.

"Who are you?" This time it was Norval who spoke.

Again a pause. Then there came a voice, grating and metallic, void of all inflection, haste, or passion, but clear and intelligible, like written words.

"George Villiers, Duke of Buckingham, I was called on earth."

" These ladies wish to hear you speak."

Van Knyper's cigarette went out. The skull turned slowly once around upon the platter. It stopped again when facing Norval; and the actor and the skull looked at one another. Then the skull turned back a quarter of a quadrant, so that it faced Mrs. de Monégo.

"And you, too, lady, wish to hear me speak?"

Mrs. de Monégo made a motion of the head; whether a nod or not, I could not tell. The death's-head took it for such, and went on.

"Of my life you know, I suppose." He said this without the least semblance of conceit. "But of my death, you, and those who are like you, have never heard."

Mrs. de Monégo made an effort. "I have heard that you were assass —— I beg your pardon," she concluded, feeling the reference to the manner of his death might be unpleasant.

"You have heard that I was assassinated. *I will begin there.*" Mrs. de Monégo pulled out a flask of smelling-salts. The death's-head went on speaking.

"Three days of respite were allowed me after dying. While the dead are still upon the surface of the earth, they are not conscious. First of all, when I came to myself, I felt an utter, close, and silent darkness; that was all. I knew not where I was. My senses were as keen as ever, but I could not see. I could not move my limbs to feel. There was no sound. When first my fearful fancy told me where I was, it was the sense of smell that guided it.

But do I shock you?" The lady to whom he had addressed his remarks had made a slight sign of disgust.

"Not at all," said she; "pray go on."

" And," said I, " if you would kindly speak not so entirely in iambics, it would be less monotonous."

The skull proceeded sternly, as if it thought me flippant. The fact is I was only frightened.

"I tell you, then, when I came back to consciousness (for that poor and earthly consciousness of mortals I, and those who live my life, can never lose), I was only conscious of black silence and eternity. In the beginning, there was not even dread. The worst I feared was the long *ennui* of infinite time. And so for many days I thought of little, for I cared for nothing; I was, and that was all; I was, and I had thought that I should cease to be. But then, one day or night, the earthy dampness told me of the grave. I could have shrieked aloud when this thought came to me. I say, I could have shrieked aloud; I did shriek, but I did not know it then. We who are dead do not know the sights and sounds our horror bids us make. This is the purport of our cries, the wailings that you hear in lonely places. But many another night, my soul, or what on earth I had called my soul, would thrill with horror at the cry of some dead body, lying near myself, who woke, as I did, and found itself still conscious in the grave. If I had ever thought of death, it was of oblivion; I had flattered myself with cowardly night; hell and

heaven were but idle words on earth, and are so still
to such as me. But this, this horror, I had not fore-
seen. I, too, was a materialist, and thought that
one could die ; forgetting, as you all forget, that
matter, by your own creed, must be eternal like the
soul. The chemicals that change in living bodies
feel and know ; why not the chemicals that change
in slow decay?

"But I can see and hear and taste still, like you
mortals ; both the flowers on your table· and the
bouquet of your wines. These five senses were all
I had cherished in my life, and the pride of my fair
body ; and now that I am dead, I am doomed to
never more leave the body, to go where it goes, and
I have the torture of the senses still. Those senses I
had cherished in my mortal frame, and kept alive for
pleasure's sake alone, are all of me that is not mortal.
You have heard how Descartes placed the locus of the
soul in the pineal gland : one single point of contact
that they have in common, where the realms of matter
and of spirit touch. Whether I have a soul I know
not ; that dread uncertainty is still one of my punish-
ments. But my consciousness is here, in this my
skull ; and it suffers but the keener agony that the
clumsy vehicles of nerve and membrane all are gone.
I, and all that is me, am chained to this dead bone ;
I cannot leave it ; I must go where it is taken ; I must
stay where this decaying matter stays. But, by the
blue sky of day, it is terrible. There were we all
together — you have heard these lines? They were

written by some poor poet of Paris, whom I used to read and like :

> " 'Now they are dead; God keep their souls!
> As to the bodies, they are rotten.
>   Lords, knaves, and ladies, in their holes
> They lie, both high and low begotten.
>   What though frumenty, cream or rice
> Fed them alive ?   The graves dissolve them ;
>   They find in these nor rice nor spice —
> May't please sweet Jesus to absolve them ! '

" There came one night or day — I know not which — when I became conscious that my body was decaying. My body I had loved so much, and had so tended with my baths and essences, my flesh too often fed by me on earth, was a thing of horror to me now; first, the eyes went, but I still saw it all; for it was only my eyes that could not see in the darkness; my soul, or what I call my soul, could see. Then the thing began on the flesh and finer membranes; but my rich dress and laces still kept fresh, as if in mockery, when all the rest was adipocere. For many days I had heard a slight grating in the wood above my eyes, and finally a clot of dust fell on my face and I saw, O living men and women —"

And here it set up such a cry of horror that all my pulses sent the blood in shivers to my heart. The women shrieked in unison, and I saw Mrs. de Monégo turn whiter than her own pearl powders.

" I beg pardon," said the skull. " I did not mean to frighten these ladies. I forgot that they are not yet familiar with these things."

Oh, the terror of that *yet!*

"I will say no more of this. You all perhaps have seen that great picture in the convent there at Seville — was it a Zurbaran or a Murillo?—where the cardinal lies in his coffin with his crimson robes and his bright jewels, and all around them — enough, I say no more. But, mind you, I could no more escape from this, dead, than you could, living. Why should we, indeed? We, who live in the lust of the eyes and the pride of life and the lust of the flesh. It is we, not heaven, who have willed these things and taken them as our portion of eternal being. For this alone I know of truth : each man may have immortal what part of himself he will. With the good comes the evil; with the joy comes the pain."

Mrs. de Monégo yawned. If it was but a sermon, she could stand it, after all. The ghost felt that he was marring his effect, and went on quickly.

"Some choose to be souls, and some to be but bodies forever. It is astonishing how many of them there were bodies besides me. For I was buried in Westminster Abbey."

The skull made this remark without a trace of pride ; but Mrs. de Monégo was reminded that she had yawned to a duke. "And how did your Grace escape from there?" said she.

Buckingham turned upon her fiercely, and his reply should have filled her with horror.

"Is there then nothing beneath the sunny side of the soil? You, who think of this fair surface as if it were always to be yours, reflect ! You laugh and dance above the earth ; your life is free and full of animal pleasure ; your neck is fair to see; no lines of grisly bone are yet in that white roundness—" (Mrs. de Monégo was certainly outrageously *décolletée*, and as the skull spoke, she drew her opera cloak about her shoulders, not used to hearing them praised in so much company.) " But think what that fair body will become, festering in the earth, hidden from sight like some foul secret crime. How did I escape, you ask ? Are there no moles ? No pipes and sewers ? No rats ? I, who speak to you, lay many score years beneath Westminster Abbey, hearing but the shriek of those who woke to find them dead. I feared — great heaven, how I feared !—that this, and this alone, might last for all eternity. The massive stone walls of my tomb seemed to promise such a fate. But finally the stones were pried aside, turned by some piercing creature, unknown to naturalists above the earth, and I was borne many miles through the ground. At last, one dark night, a mole threw me out upon the earth. Some beggar picked me up and sold me for a shilling to a student's use—I, the Duke of Buckingham. I could have read him a lesson worth many a shilling, had I been able then to speak.

" I was put in a box, and kept for many months. Of course, I could see nothing. Finally, I felt myself being moved ; apparently, from the swinging motion, I was being carried through the streets, for I could hear the rumble of carriages and smell the familiar

London paving-stones.   Then, at an interval of some
six hours, I felt that I was being moved again.   My
box was opened, and I was thrown upon a heap of
dry earth.   I was in a kind of trap-door in the floor ;
but, looking up, I could see the flies and lights of a
theatre.   In a few moments (I knew the cue) the first
grave-digger shoveled me up, and I fell and rolled
upon a stage.

   "It was a great theatre ; greater than I ever had
seen in my lifetime.   I do not know what year this
is ; but if, as I estimate, I have been dead some
eighteen hundred years, this, I think, happened about
two-thirds of the time I have been dead ago — say
about the twenty-ninth century. For twelve hundred
years I had been lying in the earth below the Abbey ;
and even in my box, these last few weeks, I had seen
no light.   And then I was suddenly thrown in the
centre of a vast and brilliant theatre, in the full glare
of the footlights.   All around in front of me were
the concentric circles of the playgoers, gay ladies, like
yourselves, in flashing jewels, and gallants leaning over
their chairs, looking at me through their eyeglasses and
taking snuff.   It seemed to me that every eye in that
great house was fixed on me, as I lay a brown, round
bone, naked and helpless in the centre of the great
bare floor, and I could see a little shudder of disgust,
and a shiver of the soft young shoulders, and their
cavaliers lean over, as if to screen them from the
shocking sight of me. Ah, well! they are all—all that
bright audience are now brown bones, as well as I.

"Once in a thousand years or so, from midnight to the sunrise, we dead are unchained from that point at the base of the skull, that we may go in spirit where we like; we may move from the place in which we lie, assume what form we choose, and speak. Once before I can remember having done so; it was at some tavern carouse, a thousand years ago in London; and it must be some memory of that, some tradition of my speaking, that has made my successive possessors keep me and treasure me with superstitious care. Is it not so?"

He turned to our host, who admitted that he had been sold to him as a very extraordinary and rare skull.

"But," said I, "your Grace mistakes. You have not yet been dead quite two hundred years."

"Is it so?" said Buckingham. "Is it indeed so?"

Here the unfortunate Mrs. de Monégo, who seemed to be always putting her foot in it when things spiritual were concerned, had a most unlucky inspiration. Meaning well (she is a woman of great social charm and always disposed to be agreeable) and thinking, perhaps, from the way the skull had kept turned toward her that it was pleased with something about her person, she drew a large red rose from her corsage, and placed it gently in the empty socket of one of Buckingham's eyes. "If your Grace can still smell, you will enjoy the fragrance," said she.

For a minute there was an awful pause. Then a voice came from the toothless jaws, not passionate or

angry, but steeped in such a Gorgon tone of horror
that its echo lingers with me yet.

"Are you not then moved yet, O woman of the
flesh? It is women such as you that lay men in
graves like mine. Know that for just so much time
as in our lives we give to things that are not of earth;
for just so much of time, in all eternity, may we escape the graves in which our petted bodies lie. And
this poor interval, when I may see the stars and
breathe the air of the sky, once in near a thousand
years, I owe to those few moments in my wretched
life on earth that I did give to things of heaven, or, at
least, to things that are not of this earth alone. Some
few moments while I lived I gave to art, to poetry,—
even of the Church I do not speak,—but those poor
minutes now are all that is given me of life in death.
Even if there be a God, I do not know, though I am
dead; nor, do I fancy, can you tell me; but these
moments, many of them already, I have given you,
that I might warn you—and you, a woman, sit there,
smiling! Do you know that with these eyes you
deem so sightless I can see things of which the fair
deceitful surface is only known to you? I see the
glitter of this table, and the painted walls—and in the
wall the coarse rubble, the refuse and plaster. I see
the carpeted floor, and beneath it the dark and filthy
soil. I see the gay streets, and in them the fever
lurking, and the germs of pestilence and seeds of
loathsome illness, madness, death, and murder. One
place is real as another, O you realists! The bowels

of the earth is as the sunshine; and you, who deem yourself so fair, so bright, so gay—in your proud body I can see each spot of gangrene, of beginning death; I can see where the blood, laden with bread, with rich food, finds some slight clot beginning in the veins; I can see all shames and blemishes you hide so secret, and each foul thought and wish that lurks, dark and deep, within your mind; I,—who might ere this have been far away in the fragrant woods and fields beneath the stars,—I have lingered here an hour to tell you this. As yet, I have learnt no more of God than you, but I have learnt that earth is death, and earth alone; and death is not oblivion: death is hell— by your own creed! He is working now, as you sit here, and all your baths and essences can keep him off but a few short years, you things of matter, as you choose to be! Death, I say; death—"

He stopped; for Mrs. de Monégo had fainted dead away. We bore her from the room. The ladies dashed water upon her, or what else; but it was many minutes before we brought her to. And finally, when we men went back to the dining-room to smoke our cigars, the skull was silent.

Norval turned to it again and tried to make it speak, but the night was nearly over, and, long ere this, its wearied spirit had escaped, and borne itself upon the air, far off, to some sweet summer sunrise in the country hills.

December.

Mrs. Knollys.

TO BE READ BY A WOOD FIRE, SOME DECEMBER EVENING.

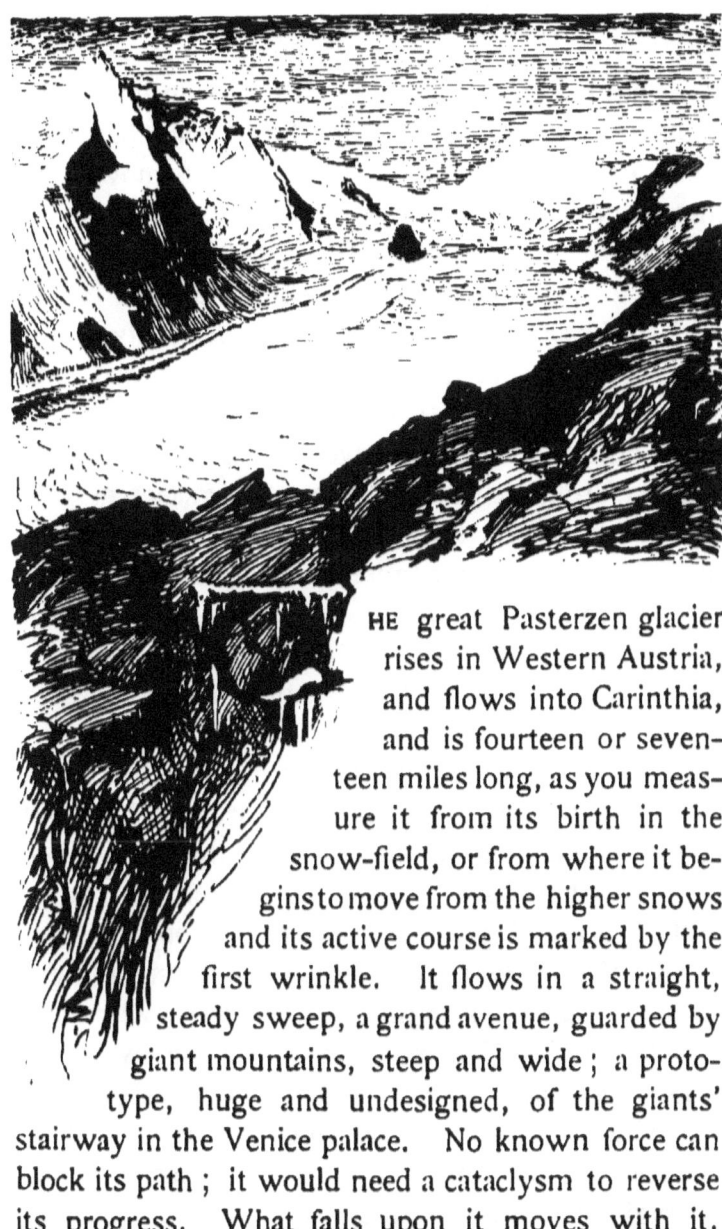

HE great Pasterzen glacier rises in Western Austria, and flows into Carinthia, and is fourteen or seventeen miles long, as you measure it from its birth in the snow-field, or from where it begins to move from the higher snows and its active course is marked by the first wrinkle. It flows in a straight, steady sweep, a grand avenue, guarded by giant mountains, steep and wide ; a prototype, huge and undesigned, of the giants' stairway in the Venice palace. No known force can block its path ; it would need a cataclysm to reverse its progress. What falls upon it moves with it,

what lies beneath it moves with it — down to the
polished surface of the earth's frame, laid bare ; no
blade of grass grows so slowly as it moves, no
meteor of the air is so irresistible.   Its substant ice
curls freely, moulds, and breaks itself like water—
breaks in waves, plastic like honey, crested lightly
with a frozen spray ; it winds tenderly about the
ro:ky shore, and the granite, disintegrated into
crumbs, flows on with it.   All this so silently that
busy, officious little Man lived a score of thousand
years before he noticed even that the glacier moved.

Now, however, men have learned to congregate
upon its shores, and admire.   Scientists stick staves
in the ground (not too near, lest the earth should
move with it), and appraise the majesty of its motion ;
ladies, politely mystified, give little screams of pleased
surprise ; young men, secretly exultant, pace the
yard or two between the sticks, a distance that takes
the frozen stream a year to compass, and look out
upon it half contemptuously.   Then they cross it —
carefully, they have enough respect left for that —
with their cunningly nailed shoes and a rope ; an hour
or two they dally with it, till at last, being hungry
and cold, they walk to the inn for supper. At supper
they tell stories of their prowess, pay money to the
guides who have protected them, and fall asleep after
tea with weariness.   Meantime, the darkness falls
outside ; but the white presence of the glacier breaks
the night, and strange shapes unseen of men dance
in its ashen hollows.   It is so old that the realms of

death and life conflict ; change is on the surface, but immortality broods in the deeper places. The moon rises and sinks; the glacier moves silently, like a time-piece marking the centuries, grooving the record of its being on the world itself — a feature to be read and studied by far-off generations of some other world. The glacier has a light of its own, and gleams to stars above, and the Great Glockner mountain flings his shadow of the planets in its face.

Mrs. Knollys was a young English bride, sunny-haired, hopeful-eyed, with lips that parted to make you love them — parted before they smiled, and all the soft regions of her face broke into attendant dimples. And then, lest you should think it meant for you, she looked quickly up to ''Charles,'' as she would then call him, even to strangers, and Charles looked down to her. Charles was a short foot taller, with much the same hair and eyes, thick, flossy whiskers, broad shoulders, and a bass voice. This was in the days before political economy cut Hymen's wings. Charles, like Mary, had little money but great hopes ; and he was clerk in a government office, with a friendly impression of everybody and much trust in himself. And old Harry Colquhoun, his chief, had given them six weeks to go to Switzerland and be happy in, all in celebration of Charles Knollys's majority and marriage to his young wife. So they had both forgotten heaven for the nonce, having a passable substitute ; but the powers divine overlooked them pleasantly and forgave it. And even the phlegmatic driver of their *Einspanner* looked back from the corner of his eye at the *schone Englan-derin*, and compared her mentally with the far-famed beauty of the Königssee. So they rattled on in their curious conveyance, with the pole in the middle and the one horse out on one side, and still found more beauty in each other's eyes than in the world about them. Although Charles was only one and twenty, Mary Knollys was barely eighteen, and to her he seemed godlike in his age, as in all other things. Her life had been as simple as it had been short. She remembered being a little girl, and then the next thing that occurred was Charles Knollys, and positively the next thing she remembered of importance was being Mrs. Charles Knollys ; so that old Mrs. Knollys, her guardian aunt and his, had first called her a love of a baby, and then but a baby in love. All this, of course, was five and forty years ago, for you know how old she was when she went again to Switzer-land last summer — three and sixty.

They first saw the great mountains from the sum-mit of the Schafberg. This is a little height, three cornered, between three lakes ; a natural Belvedere for Central Europe. Mr. and Mrs. Knollys were seated on a couch of Alpine roses behind a rhododen-dron bush watching the sunset; but as Charles was desirous of kissing Mrs. Knollys, and the rhododen-dron bush was not thick enough, they were waiting for the sun to go down. He was very slow in doing this, and by way of consolation Knollys was keeping his wife's hand hidden in the folds of her dress. Undoubtedly a modern lady would have been talking of the scenery, giving word-color pictures of the view; but I am afraid Mrs. Knollys had been looking at her husband, and talking with him of the cottage they had bought in a Surrey village, not far from Box Hill, and thinking how the little carvings and embroideries would look there which they had bought abroad. And, indeed, Mrs. Charles secretly thought Box Hill an eminence far preferable to the Venediger, and Charles's face an infinitely more interesting sight than any lake, however expressive. But the sun, looking askance at them through the lower mist, was not jealous; all the same he spread his glory lavishly for them, and the bright little mirror of a lake twinkled cannily upward from below. Finally, it grew dark; then there was less talking. It was full night when they went in, she leaning on his arm and looking up; and the moonbeam on the snowy shoulder of the Glockner, twenty leagues away, came over straightway from the mountain to her face. Three days later, Charles Knollys, crossing with her the lower portion of the Pasterzen glacier, slipped into a crevasse, and vanished utterly from the earth.

II.

ALL this you know.   And I was also told more of
the young girl, bride and widow at eighteen ; how
she sought to throw herself into the clear blue gulf;
how she refused to leave Heiligenblut ; how she
would sit, tearless, by the rim of the crevasse, day
after day, and gaze into its profundity.   A guide or
man was always with her at these times, for it was
still feared that she would follow her young husband
to the depths of that still sea.   Her aunt went over
from England to her ; the summer waxed ; autumn
storms set in ; but no power could win her from the
place whence Charles had gone.

If there was a time worse for her than that first
moment, it was when they told her that his body
never could be found.   They did not dare to tell her
this for many days, but busied themselves with idle
cranes and ladders, and made futile pretenses with
ropes.   Some of the big, simple-hearted guides even
descended into the chasm, absenting themselves for
an hour or so, to give her an idea that something
was being done.   Poor Mrs. Knollys would have
followed them had she been allowed, to wander
through the purple galleries, calling Charles.   It was
well she could not ; for all Kaspar could do was to
lower himself a hundred yards or so, chisel out a
niche, and stand in it, smoking his honest pipe to
pass the time, and trying to fancy he could hear the
murmur of the waters down below.   Meantime Mrs.

Knollys strained her eyes, peering downward from above, leaning on the rope about her waist, looking over the clear brink of the bergschrund.

It was the Herr Doctor Zimmermann who first told her the truth. Not that the good Doctor meant to do so. The Herr Doctor had had his attention turned to glaciers by some rounded stones in his garden by the Traunsee, and more particularly by the Herr Privatdocent Splûthner. Splûthner, like Uncle Toby, had his hobby-horse, his pet conjuring words, his gods *ex machinâ*, which he brought upon the field in scientific emergencies; and these gods, as with Thales, were Fire and Water. Craters and flood were his accustomed scape-goats, upon whose heads were charged the unaccountable; and the Herr Doctor, who had only one element left to choose from, and that a passive one, but knew, on general principles, that Splûthner must be wrong, got as far off as he could and took Ice. And Splûthner having pooh-poohed this, Zimmermann rode his hypothesis with redoubled zeal. He became convinced that ice was the embodiment of orthodoxy. Fixing his professional spectacles on his substantial nose, he went into Carinthia and ascended the great Venice mountains, much as he would have performed any other scientific experiment. Then he encamped on the shores of the Pasterzen glacier, and proceeded to make a study of it.

So it happened that the Doctor, taking a morning stroll over the subject of his experiment, in search of

small things which might verify his theory, met Mrs.
Knollys sitting in her accustomed place. The Doctor had been much puzzled, that morning, on finding
in a rock at the foot of the glacier the impression, or
sign-manual as it were, of a certain Fish, whose acquaintance the Doctor had previously made only in
tropical seas. This fact seeming, superficially, to
chime in with Splüthnerian mistakes in a most het-
erodox way, the Doctor's mind had for a moment
been diverted from the ice ; and he was wondering
what the fish had been going to do in that particular
gallery, and secretly doubting whether it had known
its own mind, and gone thither with the full knowledge and permission of its maternal relative. Indeed,
the good Doctor would probably have ascribed its
presence to the malicious and personal causation of
the devil, but that the one point on which he and
Splüthner were agreed was the ignoring of unscientific
hypotheses. The Doctor's objections to the devil
were none the less strenuous for being purely scientific.

Thus ruminating, the Doctor came to the crevasse
where Mrs. Knollys was sitting, and to which a little
path had now been worn from the inn. There was
nothing of scientific interest about the fair young
English girl, and the Doctor did not notice her ; but
he took from his waistcoat-pocket a leaden bullet,
moulded by himself, and marked "Johannes Carpen-
tarius, Juvavianus, A. U. C. 2590," and dropped it,
with much satisfaction, into the crevasse. Mrs.

Knollys gave a little cry; the bullet was heard for some seconds tinkling against the sides of the chasm; the tinkles grew quickly fainter, but they waited in vain for the noise of the final fall. " May the Splüthner live that he may learn by it," muttered the Doctor; " I can never recover it."

Then he remembered that the experiment had been attended with a sound unaccounted for by the conformity of the bullet to the laws of gravitation; and looking up, he saw Mrs. Knollys in front of him, no longer crying, but very pale. Zimmermann started, and in his confusion dropped his best brass registering thermometer, which also rattled down the abyss.

" You say," whispered Mrs. Knollys, " that it can never be recovered ! "

" Madam," spoke the Doctor, doffing his hat, " how would you recofer from a blace when the smallest approximation which I haf yet been able to make puts the depth from the surface to the bed of the gletscher at vrom sixteen hundred to sixteen hundred and sixty *mètres* in distance?" Doctor Zimmermann spoke very good English; and he pushed his hat upon the back of his head, and assumed his professional attitude.

" But they all were trying —" Mrs. Knollys spoke faintly. " They said that they hoped he could be recovered." The stranger was the oldest gentleman she had seen, and Mrs. Knollys felt almost like confiding in him. " Oh, I must have the — the body." She closed in a sob; but the Herr Doctor caught at the last word, and this suggested to him only the language of scientific experiment.

"Recofer it? If, madam," Zimmermann went on with all the satisfaction attendant on the enunciation of a scientific truth, "we take a body and drop it in the schrund of this gletscher; and the ice-stream moves so slower at its base than on the upper part, and the ice will cover it; efen if we could reach the base, which is a mile in depth. Then, see you, it is all caused by the motion of the ice —"

But at this Mrs. Knollys had given a faint cry, and her guide rushed up angrily to the old professor, who stared helplessly forward. "God will help me, sir," said she to the Doctor, and she gave the guide her arm and walked wearily away.

The professor still stared, in amazement at her enthusiasm for scientific experiment and the passion with which she greeted his discoveries. Here was a person who utterly refused to be referred to the agency of Ice, or even, like Splûthner, of Fire and Water; and went out of the range of allowable hypotheses to call upon a Noumenon. Now both Splûthner and Zimmermann had studied all natural agencies and made allowance for them, but for the Divine they had always hitherto proved an alibi. The Doctor could make nothing of it.

At the inn that evening he saw Mrs. Knollys with swollen eyes; and remembering the scene of the afternoon, he made inquiries about her of the inn-keeper. The latter had heard the guide's account of the meeting ; and as soon as Zimmermann had made plain what he had told her of the falling body, "Triple blockhead!" said he. "*Es war ihr Mann.*" The Herr Professor staggered back into his seat ; and the kindly innkeeper ran upstairs to see what had happened to his poor young guest.

Mrs. Knollys had recovered from the first shock by this time, but the truth could no longer be withheld. The innkeeper could but nod his head sadly when she told him that to recover her Charles was hopeless. All the guides said the same thing. The poor girl's husband had vanished from the world as utterly as if his body had been burned to ashes and scattered in the pathway of the winds. Charles Knollys was gone, utterly gone ; no more to be met with by his girl-wife, save as spirit to spirit, soul to soul, in ultramundane place. The fair-haired young Englishman lived but in her memory, as his soul, if still existent, lived in places indeterminate, unknowable to Doctor Zimmermann and his compeers. Slowly Mrs. Knollys acquired the belief that she was never to see her Charles again. Then, at last, she resolved to go — to go home. Her strength now gave way ; and when her aunt left, she had with her but the ghost of Mrs. Knollys — a broken figure, drooping in the carriage, veiled in black. The innkeeper and all the guides stood bare-headed, silent, about the door, as the carriage drove off, bearing the bereaved widow back to England.

III.

WHEN the Herr Doctor had heard the innkeeper's answer, he sat for some time with his hands planted on his knees, looking through his spectacles at the opposite wall. Then he lifted one hand and struck his brow impatiently. It was his way, when a chemical reaction had come out wrong.

"Du Dummkopf!" said he. "Triple blockhead, thou art so bad as Splüthner." No self-condemnation could have been worse to him than this. Thinking again of Mrs. Knollys, he gave one deep, gruff sob. Then he took his hat, and, going out, wandered by the shore of the glacier in the night, repeating to himself the Englishwoman's words: "*They said that they hoped he could be recovered.*" Zimmermann came to the tent where he kept his instruments, and stood there, looking at the sea of ice. He went to his measuring pegs, two rods of iron : one sunk deep and frozen in the glacier, the other drilled into a rock on the shore. "Triple blockhead!" said he again ; "thou art worse than Splüthner. The Splüthner said the glacier did not move ; thou, thou knowest that it does." He sighted from his rods to the mountain opposite. There was a slight and all but imperceptible change of direction from the day before.

He could not bear to see the English girl again, and all the next day was absent from the inn. For a month he stopped at Heiligenblut, and busied himself with his instruments. The guides of the place greeted him coldly every day, as they started on their glacier excursions or their chamois hunting. But none the less did Zimmermann return the following summer, and work upon his great essay in refutation of the Splüthner.

Mrs. Knollys went back to the little cottage in Surrey, and lived there. The chests and cases she brought back lay unopened in the store-room : the little rooms of the cottage that was to be their home remained bare and unadorned, as Charles had seen them last. She could not bring herself to alter them now. What she had looked forward to do with him she had no strength to do alone. She rarely went out. There was no place where she could go to think of him. He was gone ; gone from England, gone from the very surface of the earth. If he had only been buried in some quiet English church-yard, she thought,— some green place lying open to the sun, where she could go and scatter flowers on his grave, where she could sit and look forward amid her tears to the time when she should lie side by side with him,— they would then be separated for her short life alone. Now it seemed to her that they were far apart forever.

But late the next summer she had a letter from the place. It was from Dr. Zimmermann. There is no need here to trace the quaint German phrases, the formalism, the cold terms of science in which he made his meaning plain. It spoke of erosion ; of the

movement of the summer ; of the action of the under-
waters on the ice.   And it told her, with tender
sympathy oddly blended with the pride of scientific
success, that he had given a year's most careful study
to the place ; with all his instruments of measure-
ment he had tested the relentless glacier's flow ;
and it closed by assuring her that her husband might
yet be found—in five and forty years.   In five and
forty years,—the poor professor staked his scientific reputation on the fact,—in five and forty years
she might return, and the glacier would give up its
dead.

This letter made Mrs. Knollys happier.   It made
her willing to live ; it made her almost long to live
until old age — that her Charles's body might be
given back.   She took heart to beautify her little
home.   The trifling articles she had bought with
Charles were now brought out—the little curiosities
and pictures he had given her on their wedding journey.   She would ask how such and such a thing
looked, turning her pretty head to some kind visitor,
as she ranged them on the walls.   Now and then she
would have to lay the picture down, and cry a little,
silently, as she remembered where Charles had told
her it would look best.   Still, she sought to furnish
the rooms as they had planned them in their mind ;
she made her surroundings, as nearly as she could,
as they had pictured them together.   One room she
never went into ; it was the room Charles had meant
to have for the nursery.   She had no child.

But she changed, as we all change, with the passing of the years. I first remember her as a woman
middle-aged, sweet-faced, hardly like a widow, nor
yet like an old maid. She was rather like a young
girl in love, with her lover absent on a long journey.
She lived more with the memory of her husband ; she
clung to him more than if she had had a child. She
never married—you would have guessed that ; but,
after the professor's letter, she never quite seemed to
realize that her husband was dead. Was he not
coming back to her?

Never in all my knowledge of dear English women
have I known a woman so much loved. In how
many houses was she always the most welcome
guest! How often we boys would go to her for
sympathy! I know she was the confidante of all our
love affairs. I cannot speak for girls ; but I fancy she
was much the same with them. Many of us owed
our life's happiness to her. She would chide us
gently in our pettiness and folly, and teach us, by
her very presence and example, what thing it was
that alone could keep life sweet. How well we all
remember the little Surrey cottage, the little home
fireside where the husband had never been ! I think
she grew to imagine his presence, even the presence
of children : boys, curly-headed, like Charles, and
sweet, blue-eyed daughters ; and the fact that it was
all imagining seemed but to make the place more
holy. Charles still lived to her as she had believed
him in the month that they were married : he lived

through life with her as her young love had fancied
he would be.   She never thought of evil that might
have occurred—of failing affection, of cares.   Her
happiness was in her mind alone ; so all the earthly
part was absent.

There were but two events in her life—that which
was past and that which was to come. She had lived
through his loss ; now she lived on for his recovery.
But, as I have said, she changed, as all things mortal
change ; all but the earth and the ice-stream and the
stars above it.   She read much, and her mind grew
deep and broad, none the less gentle with it all ; she
was wiser in the world ; she knew the depths of
human hope and sorrow.   You remember her only
as an old lady whom we loved.   Only her heart did
not change—I forgot that ; her heart, and the memory of that last loving smile upon his face, as he bent
down to look into her eyes, before he slipped and fell.
She lived on, and waited for his body, as possibly his
other self—who knows?—waited for hers. As she
grew older she grew taller ; her eyes were quieter,
her hair a little straighter, darker than of yore ; her
face changed, only the expression remained the same.
Mary Knollys !

Human lives rarely look more than a year, or five,
ahead ; Mary Knollys looked five and forty.   Many
of us wait, and grow weary in waiting, for those
few years alone, and for some living friend.   Mary
Knollys waited five and forty years—for the dead.
Still, after that first year, she never wore all black ;

only silvery grays, and white with a black ribbon or two. I have said that she almost seemed to think her husband living. She would fancy his doing this and that with her ; how he would joy in this good fortune, or share her sorrows — which were few, mercifully. His memory seemed to be a living thing to her, to go through life with her, hand in hand. It changed as she grew old ; it altered itself to suit her changing thought, until the very memory of her memory seemed to make it sure that he had really been alive with her, really shared her happiness or sorrow, in the far-off days of her earliest widowhood. It hardly seemed that he had been gone already then — she remembered him so well. She could not think that he had never been with her in their little cottage. And now, at sixty, I know she thought of him as an old person too ; sitting by their fireside, late in life, mature, deep-souled, wise with the wisdom of years, going back with her, fondly, to recall the old, old happiness of their bridal journey, when they set off for the happy honeymoon abroad, and the long life now past stretched brightly out before them both. She never spoke of this, and you children never knew it ; but it was always in her mind.

There was a plain stone in the little Surrey church-yard, now gray and moss-grown with the rains of forty years, on which you remember reading : "Charles Knollys — lost in Carinthia —— " This was all she would have inscribed ; he was but lost :

no one *knew* that he was dead.   Was he not yet to be found?   There was no grassy mound beside it; the earth was smooth.   Not even the date was there. But Mrs. Knollys never went to read it.   She waited until he should come ; until that last journey, re- peating the travels of their wedding-days, when she should go to Germany to bring him home.

So the woman's life went on in England, and the glacier in the Alps moved on slowly ; and the woman waited for it to be gone.

IV.

In the summer of 1882, the little Carinthian village of Heiligenblut was haunted by two persons.   One was a young German scientist, with long hair and specta- cles ; the other was a tall English lady slightly bent, with a face wherein the finger of time had deeply written tender things.   Her hair was white as silver, and she wore a long, black veil.   Their habits were strangely similar.   Every morning, when the eastern light shone deepest into the ice-cavern at the base of the great Pasterzen glacier, these two would walk thither ; then both would sit for an hour or two and peer into its depths.   Neither knew why the other was there.   The woman would go back for an hour in the late afternoon ; the man, never.   He knew that the morning light was necessary for his search.

The man was the famous young Zimmermann, son of his father, the old Doctor, long since dead. But the Herr Doctor had written a famous tract, when late in life, refuting all Splüthners, past, present, and to come; and had charged his son, in his dying moments, as a most sacred trust, that he should repair to the base of the Pasterzen glacier in the year 1882, where he would find a leaden bullet, graven with his father's name, and the date A. U. C. 2590. All this would be vindication of his father's science. Splüthner, too, was a very old man, and Zimmermann the younger (for even he was no longer young) was fearful lest Splüthner should not live to witness his own refutation. The woman and the man never spoke to each other.

Alas, no one could have known Mrs. Knollys for the fair English girl who had been there in the young days of the century; not even the innkeeper, had he been there. But he, too, was long since dead. Mrs. Knollys was now bent and white-haired; she had forgotten, herself, how she had looked in those old days. Her life had been lived. She was now like a woman of another world; it seemed another world in which her fair hair had twined about her husband's fingers, and she and Charles had stood upon the evening mountain, and looked in one another's eyes. That was the world of her wedding-days, but it seemed more like a world she had left when born on earth. And now he was coming back to her in this. Meantime the great Pasterzen

glacier had moved on, marking only the centuries ;
the men upon its borders had seen no change ; the
same great waves lifted their snowy heads upon its
surface ; the same crevasse still was where he had
fallen.   At night, the moonbeams, falling, still shiv-
ered off its glassy face ; its pale presence filled the
night, and immortality lay brooding in its hollows.

Friends were with Mrs. Knollys, but she left them
at the inn.   One old guide remembered her, and
asked to bear her company.   He went with her in
the morning, and sat a few yards from her, waiting.
In the afternoon she went alone.   He would not
have credited you, had you told him that the glacier
moved.   He thought it but an Englishwoman's
fancy, but he waited with her.   Himself had never
forgotten that old day.   And Mrs. Knollys sat there
silently, searching the clear depths of the ice, that she
might find her husband.

One night she saw a ghost.   The latest beam of
the sun, falling on a mountain opposite, had shone
back into the ice-cavern ; and seemingly deep within,
in the grave azure light, she fancied she saw a face
turned towards her.   She even thought she saw
Charles's yellow hair, and the self-same smile his
lips had worn when he bent down to her before he
fell.   It could be but a fancy.   She went home, and
was silent with her friends about what had happened.   In the moonlight she went back, and again
the next morning before dawn.   She told no one of
her going ; but the old guide met her at the door,

and walked silently behind her. She had slept, the glacier ever present in her dreams.

The sun had not yet risen when she came ; and she sat a long time in the cavern, listening to the murmur of the river, flowing under the glacier at her feet. Slowly the dawn began, and again she seemed to see the shimmer of a face — such a face as one sees in the coals of a dying fire. Then the full sun came over the eastern mountain, and the guide heard a woman's cry. There before her was Charles Knollys ! The face seemed hardly pale ; and there was the same faint smile — a smile like her memory of it, five and forty years gone by. Safe in the clear ice, still, unharmed, there lay — O God ! not her Charles ; not the Charles of her own thought, who had lived through life with her and shared her sixty years ; not the old man she had borne thither in her mind — but a boy, a boy of one and twenty lying asleep, a ghost from another world coming to confront her from the distant past, immortal in the immortality of the glacier. There was his quaint coat, of the fashion of half a century before ; his blue eyes open ; his young, clear brow ; all the form of the past she had forgotten ; and she his bride stood there to welcome him, with her wrinkles, her bent figure, and thin white hairs. She was living, he was dead ; and she was two and forty years older than he.

Then at last the long-kept tears came to her, and she bent her white head in the snow. The old man came up with his pick, silently, and began working in the ice. The woman lay weeping, and the boy, with his still, faint smile, lay looking at them, through the clear ice-veil, from his open eyes.

I believe that the professor found his bullet; I know not. I believe that the scientific world rang with his name and the thesis that he published on the glacier's motion, and the changeless temperature his father's lost thermometer had shown. All this you may read. I know no more.

But I know that in the English church-yard there are now two graves, and a single stone, to Charles Knollys and Mary, his wife ; and the boy of one and twenty sleeps there with his bride of sixty-three ; his young frame with her old one, his yellow hair beside her white. And I do not know that there is not some place, not here, where they are still together, and he is twenty-one and she is still eighteen. I do not know this ; but I know that all the pamphlets of the German doctor cannot tell me it is false.

Meantime the great Pasterzen glacier moves on, and the rocks with it ; and the mountain flings his shadow of the planets in its face.

THE END.